Deadly Game

Deadly Game

The Horns of the Rhino

Dr. Robert E. Marx

Prominent Books

Editing: Writer Services, LLC (WriterServices.net)
Cover Design & Book Layout: Writer Services, LLC

ISBN-10: 1-942389-24-8
ISBN-13: 978-1-942389-24-8

TABLE OF CONTENTS

Dr. Marx paints a vivid picture of troubled times in the beautiful lands of Africa. His unfailing attention to detail brings the reader out of his chair and into the scene. In "The Horns of the Rhino", Dr. Marx fully reclaims for us all medicine as an art form and threads that art form throughout this compelling tale of the challenges of humanity and nature.

Timothy M. O'Brien, Senior Partner, Levin Papantonio, P.A.

Dedication

This book is dedicated to the Black and White Rhinoceros in the hope that the enlightened next generation of those in Asian countries and those of the Asian culture will abandon the false notion that powdered rhinoceros horn has any medicinal or aphrodisiac properties.

It is also dedicated to the elephant herds on two continents in the hope that the collectors and the elite worldwide would cease their desire for ornaments derived from the tusks (which are actually teeth) of these endangered and majestic animals.

This book is further dedicated to Kruger National Park as well as the other national parks and the private game camps throughout Africa. To their owners, guides, and trackers such as those in Simbambili/South Africa who educate us and protect these unique animals and their habitats daily.

Robert E. Marx
Professor of Surgery
University of Miami Miller School of Medicine.

Chapter 1
Goliath

Early September is the height of the dry season in Kruger National Park, South Africa. The seasonal rains arising from the Indian Ocean and blowing westward are not due to arrive until November. Nevertheless, sufficient water remains in the Sabi and Sand Rivers, located in the southern reaches of this Connecticut-sized area, to maintain the health of its wildlife and even attract numerous other creatures from outside the park. Yet, even in the wet season, November through April, the landscape of South Africa and its neighbor to the north, Botswana, is not the dense, green jungle portrayed in Hollywood movies but an arid stretch of scrub, plains, and scattered trees referred to as "the bush." It is this bush where the field team of young park ranger Richard Rimer and his partner Jim McCullar are assembling over a shallow ditch to act as a blind.

Rimer brings his canteen of water to his parched lips. He and McCullar rose well before dawn and, after a four-mile trek and three hours of work, are finally putting the finishing touches on their hide. He inhales deeply, taking in the musty smell of rhino urine and dung that makes up a nearby midden, the area where white rhinos go to defecate and urinate. More than just a community toilet, rhino middens are an integral and valuable part of the local ecosystem, both as a form of communication among the rhinos and to establish a hierarchy of sorts and a stamp for mating rights.

Today, though, Rimer is concerned with tracking one particularly large male white rhino who regularly contributes to the midden in order to mark his territory and let others know of his strength and dominance and, hopefully, catching the poachers seeking to slay him for his horns. For Rimer, an expert in rhino reproduction and behavior, this is not just an academic exercise but a passion project dear to his heart.

Born and raised in Lions Gate Private Safari Camp, Rimer was taking trips into the bush when other kids were still playing with blocks. He would tag along with his parents and the guides and trackers in the camp, soaking up every bit of knowledge as they took guests on their morning and late afternoon photographic game drives.

Early on, he developed a special fondness for the rhinos and would study them intensely, not only in his formal education but by pumping the camp's many trackers to learn their habits and specific traits.

By his mid-twenties, he had his Ph.D. and multiple job offers from universities and conservationist groups, but his goal had always been to become a park ranger. He remembered vividly the first day he dressed in those khaki shorts, a matching short-sleeved shirt with a park ranger patch on the left breast pocket, and a green baseball cap. It was one of the proudest moments of his life, the other being the day the South African government asked him to take place in its most recent efforts to quell the rising incidence of poaching.

Rimer hands the canteen to McCullar, who accepts it with a grunt. It is the most he had said in hours, but Rimer doesn't mind; he cannot imagine they would have much to talk about. Whereas Rimer is a slight, bespectacled geek more comfortable with books than people, "Big Jim" McCullar is thick-bodied, six-foot-four Australian known equally for his skills as a rugby player and mercenary for hire. After years of wet work in Angola, Syria and Turkey, his reputation as a rugged outdoorsman and a crack shot with every weapon from handguns to AK-47s attracted the attention of the newly commissioned anti-poaching administration.

"I think we're about done," McCullar says after taking a long pull from the canteen. Rimer surveys their handiwork—thorny branches from numerous acacia trees and four-foot spikes made from dense leadwood branches—and nods. It is time to settle in and await their quarry. For the first time, they notice the constant bip-bip-birr of the ubiquitous cape doves as well as the shrill chatter and rustling of vervet monkeys in the trees. They also occasionally hear the distant echoing roar of two pride male lions. Neither is particularly concerned about the lions' roar—Rimer, because his field experience tells him the pride is at least five miles away and that these two pride males, probably brothers, are merely letting other males know of their whereabouts and warning them not to trespass on their territory or threaten their young and lionesses; Jim McCullar, because he is clutching his .458

caliber rifle, also known as an elephant gun; he also has at his disposal a 9mm Glock, a machete, and two nine-inch knives sheathed in his belt and ready at a moment's notice. Rimer glances at the weapons, knowing that Big Jim is there to protect him, not so much from the dangerous "big five" animals such as elephants, cape buffalo, lions, leopards and rhinos, but from the ruthless poachers who have had no qualms about killing park rangers right along with their four-legged prey recently.

"Hey, mate, this rhino we're supposed to save, is it white or black?"

"White," Rimer replies. "There are only a few black rhinos left. Poachers have killed most of them, and they're less reproductive than whites."

"Well, you certainly know a lot about these creatures. Which one is bigger and has the bigger horns?"

"The white rhino by far, Jim. Black rhinos rarely weigh more than 1400 kilograms, whereas white rhinos can get up to 3200. Their horns relate to their body size."

"So mate, the rhino of this adventure is a big white boy, eh?"

Rimer peers at McCullar through his field sunglasses. "Sure is. I've been following Goliath—that's what I call him—for the past two years. He's the biggest rhino I've ever seen and has the biggest horn I've ever seen. That's why he is such a temptation for poachers. Our informants tell us that the poachers will make their attempt today. We are to intercept them, protect the rhino at all costs, and try to capture at least one of the poachers so he can tell us who and where his buyers are. Is that clear, Mr. McCullar?"

"Crystal clear, mate, but just call me Big Jim. So what's so valuable about the rhino horn anyhow?"

"You really don't know?" asks Rimer with an incredulous look. "Well, it actually has no real biologic or medicinal value. It is composed entirely of keratin, which is the same protein that makes up your fingernails, and the filtering system of most whales called Baleen."

"Boy, you're a smart one, aren't ya?"

Rimer continues, not quite sure if Big Jim is complimenting or insulting him. "It is believed to be a male sexual enhancer and an aphrodisiac as well as an all-around medicine by the Asian and Southeast Asian cultures. It is ground up into a powder and given to most all Chinese men on their wedding night and used extensively in the oriental sex trade."

Big Jim's eyes widen, his first sign of real interest. "And does it work?"

"Heck no! It only works because their traditions and cultures tell those taking it that it does." Rimer shakes his head in disgust. "It's only a placebo, and, for that, a beautiful animal has to be killed."

"I agree with ya there, mate. Good thing Big Jim doesn't need anything to enhance his performance. Heck, just the other night, I outlasted two native girls in Joburg. I could've taken on a third, but I ran out of rands and they wouldn't take a credit card."

Rimer shakes his head, hoping Big Jim is as talented a solider as he is a womanizer. "Okay, Jim, time to talk about the plan. Goliath comes around to mark the midden right just before dark, between 5:30 and 6:30 each night. I suspect the poachers know that." Rimer gestures to their right. "They'll be hiding in the bush closest to the road over there."

"How do you know that?"

"They have been observing this rhino for the past two weeks. I found their tracks, which lead from the road south of the park to their own hide in the bush about two kilometers from us. That's why I insisted we station our hide to the west, so that we have a direct view of the midden and can see them without the sun in our eyes when they leave their hide and move into the clearing."

"No worries, Rick. I'll handle the poachers with this." McCullar points to his 458 caliber rifle.

"Hold on, Big Jim. We're to apprehend these poachers, not kill them. We want to find out who their bosses are. It's the only way to break down the trail of poaching that begins here in the bush then travels through Johannesburg and somehow gets shipped to China, Singapore, Malaysia and other countries. Besides, my own moral belief is that we have no right to kill innocent animals or people."

"Gotcha, mate, but these people are not innocent."

"You're right, but it's not for us to decide their fate; that's what the law is for."

Jim offers a noncommittal grunt, and Rimer can't help

but think the Australian is disappointed that there will be no killing that day. For the next two hours, the men sit in companionable silence, punctuated by the chatter of the vervet monkeys and an occasional howl from the dominant male in a nearby troop of baboons, as they await the anticipated arrival of the big rhino and likely the poachers as well.

Then, just as the sky is turning a fiery red, Rimer sees Goliath's massive, white body passing a stand of acacia trees on his way to the midden. He turns to McCullar to find the large Australian dozing.

"Jim," he whispers urgently, "wake up. He's here!"

Instantly alert, Jim clutches the rifle, his eyes widening at the sight of the rhino.

"You weren't kiddin', mate. That bugger's huge!"

They watch as Goliath saunters up to the pile of previously deposited rhino urine and feces. With head down, accentuating his long, massive horns, he begins to kick at the urine-soaked clumps of dung to spread it and make room for his own. He then sprays his own strong musty scent, a signal for other males to show caution and for females to be impressed with his strength and virility.

Suddenly, the three poachers emerge into the clearing, exactly where Rimer predicted they would. Before he can react, a shot rings out, and Goliath collapses straight down as if all four legs were suddenly amputated.

"Noooo!" Rimer screams, his own animal instincts urging him to run to the fallen rhino even as his human mind tells him there is nothing he can do to save him.

Three more shots ring out in rapid succession, felling each of the three poachers. In horror, Rimer looks over to Big Jim McCullar to see his eye pressed to the rifle's scope, a thick finger on the trigger. McCullar lowers the gun to the ground, then turns to Rimer, his eyes icy.

"You! You shot *Goliath*! And the poach—"

Before he can finish the sentence, McCullar grabs him by the hair, whips one of the nine-inch blades from his belt, and shoves it under Rimer's sternum. As the knife goes into his heart, Rimer tries to cry out but succeeds only in making a gurgling sound.

"Do I know about the value of rhino horns?" McCullar says mockingly. "You bet I do, mate. It's millions, and Big Jim is going to get a large chunk of it."

He then lets the limp body of Richard Rimer fall off his knife and takes out his radio. "Flying Fish, Flying Fish. This is the Wombat. Mission accomplished. Do you copy?"

"Copy that, Wombat," comes the reply from a nearby helicopter.

"Cargo will be ready in five minutes," McCullar replies. "See you then. Over and out."

With that, McCullar expertly uses his machete to chop away the thorny hide he built a few hours earlier. He then runs over to the body of one of the poachers and pries a chainsaw from the dead man's fingers before turning to the fallen rhino.

Goliath died almost instantly, a result of Jim's expert shot to its relatively small brain, but this is irrelevant to McCullar, just as he barely notices the macabre mess he makes as he runs the chainsaw through the front face of the animal. His entire focus now is on collecting his prize—the sixty-pound primary horn and its ten-pound secondary horn. He pulls on the primary horn to remove the front face, then the chainsaw comes down again, this time to separate the two horns from one another.

A moment later, McCullar hears the whirring of the approaching chopper and, tucking the horns under one burly arm, rushes toward it with his head down to protect his eyes from dust kicked up by the rotary blades. As soon as he climbs aboard, the steel bird lifts off, leaving the carcasses below to be scavenged by hyenas, jackals, or lions, who will not pass up a free meal. The whole bloody ordeal has taken less than ten minutes.

CHAPTER 2
Upwind but Down and Out

Two weeks ago, four less experienced hunters set off in search of a much larger quarry. It was just past noon when these members of the Ugandan Revolutionary Liberation Army began their quest for ivory and meat to feed their comrades. Finally, after four hours of following the trail of elephant dung and broken brush, they spot the herd. It is a female breeding herd of twenty adults and about as many juveniles. The party of four is not surprised when they see no mature bulls, as these bulls are loaners and only approach the heard for mating, but they are grateful. A testosterone-overloaded male would disrupt the herd and make the hunters' mission much more dangerous.

Choban, the group's self-appointed leader, quietly signals for the other three to circle ahead of the herd so as to get them in a crossfire. A twenty-something volunteer from Kampala on the north shore of Lake Victoria, Choban joined the RLA two years earlier after his village was pillaged by government troops.

Late one night as the people slept, troops had ridden into the village, burning most of it to the ground and killing as many men as they could. They then proceeded to rape the women, including Choban's wife and sister. Choban himself escaped by killing one of the troops with a machete and disappearing into the night with his attacker's pistol and rifle. Since then, he has proven himself an asset for the RLA—handy with a rifle, pistol, or machete and fierce in battle. He's had his fair share of kills in the numerous raids on government outposts. Today, however, would be his first elephant hunt and his most important mission to date.

Killing elephants is a far different matter than killing humans but is at least as dangerous. Choban doesn't realize this; if he had, he would have known that he and his three equally inexperienced partners are upwind of the herd and that they are moving too slowly to get into their positions before being detected. The herd draws closer amidst the low rumblings of the adult elephants and the breaking of bush and tree branches. The biggest elephant is the matriarch of the herd and clearly their leader, rumbling messages in low tones to her sisters and cousins. An occasional non-aggressive trumpeting is heard as one elephant inadvertently encroaches on the dining site of another, while oxpecker birds flirt about their backs to dine on ticks and other parasites.

The matriarch suddenly stops and raises her trunk. Sniffing the air, she catches an unpleasant and very familiar odor: human mingled with gun oil. Before she can react, Choban, sensing that he has been discovered, attempts a quick shot from his rifle. The bullet only grazes the high and prominent forehead ridge on the elephant's left side. She immediately trumpets a loud and sustained warning to the rest of her herd; the stampede has begun.

Choban struggles to reload his single-barreled rifle as the herd, now stampeding through the open clearing at twenty miles per hour and trumpeting all the way, heads for his three comrades. Frightened beyond all reason, they do not shoot to detour the oncoming herd but instead take off running—a deadly mistake. Humans, especially those dressed in military clothing and heavy, water-resistant boots, cannot outrun a stampeding herd. Choban can do nothing but watch helplessly as they are overtaken and, amidst terrifying screams and the crushing of bones and flesh, quickly meet their demise. The herd continues their running and trumpeting, unaware and uncaring about the humans reduced to bloody stains on the trampled grass behind them.

As the elephants disappear into the distance, an eerie silence takes over the clearing. Choban sinks to the ground, trying to process what has just occurred. It easily could have been him who met his death in that clearing. As the shock begins to wear off, he realizes his life is still in danger, not from the elephants but at the hands of the rebel leader when he learns of the failed mission.

Three hours later, Choban makes his way back to camp. It is dusk, with a gentle breeze stirring through the trees and a fiery red-orange sun in the western sky. This serene scene is in sharp contrast with the tense, rage-filled climate inside the thatched hut of Nobutu, the rebel leader.

"You tell me that you brought back no ivory," Nobutu snarls, "that there is no ivory out there for us to pick up tomorrow. You also tell me that there is no meat for my troops. What am I supposed to feed them? Worst of all, three of my troops are dead because of your incompetence. How can I liberate our country without an army?" His cold eyes bore into Choban's frightened ones. "You must pay for this."

"Please, Nobutu, I tried hard. The elephants were too numerous and too excited, and they ran and killed the others. I'll do kitchen duty, clean rifles, sharpen machetes, and hunt small game. Whatever you wish, just please, show mercy on me."

The moment the words leave his mouth, Choban realizes his mistake. Nobutu's jaw tightens indicating his disgust with the young soldier's display of weakness.

"Enough," Nobutu says quietly as he takes a step toward the quivering Choban. His expression softens slightly, and just when Choban thinks he might get a reprieve, the leader suddenly pulls a knife from his belt and thrusts it into the young man's chest.

Choban manages a strangled, "I'm sorry," then falls to the floor, the fourth victim of an elephant hunt gone terribly wrong.

CHAPTER 3
The Making of a Revolutionary

Nobutu Ingale was not always a merciless revolutionary; in fact, his early life was one of quiet gentility. He was born Nobutu Menga in 1969, the middle child in an upper-middle-class Ugandan family. His father, Mustafa Menga, was a successful merchant in partnership with an East Indian importer of furniture in Uganda's capital of Kampala. His mother, Nolongo, a slender, elegant woman of Nigerian extraction, divided her time between charity work and raising Nobutu, his older brother and his younger sister. The children went to the best schools and had everything they needed. However, even money and social status were not enough to protect Mustafa Menga's family from his country's tumultuous political climate.

It was the time of the brutal dictator General Idi Amin, who had seized power from Uganda's second president, Milton Obote, in January of 1971. As commander of the Ugandan army, Amin quickly established a military government and began to purge all rivals. Under the banner of "Africa for Africans" and a bitter resentment of British Colonialism, he set about murdering anyone connected to the vestiges of British rule, including the many who had immigrated from India years before. Amin's megalomania only escalated from there. Declaring himself "conqueror of the British Empire" and "His Excellency, President for Life," he threatened to annex parts of neighboring Kenya and Sudan and nationalize British-owned businesses. He also continued his murderous purges, which now targeted not only those associated with India but with people of the Acholi and Lango ethnic Ugandan tribes, the latter of which Mustafa Menga belonged.

Nobutu would never forget that day in 1977 when his life changed forever. He was eight years old and had just returned home from an afterschool football practice. The moment he saw his mother, he could see by the set of her jaw and anxious eyes that something was wrong. Even her embrace was different than usual—tighter and somehow desperate. It was then he noticed that his mother was wearing old, tattered clothes and a white headband—clothes that were usually only worn by servants.

Without an explanation, and much to his surprise, his mother told him to take off his parochial school uniform and change into his oldest play clothes. He went into his room and removed his blue shorts and white knitted shirt with his school emblem emblazed over the left pocket. He carefully folded them and dressed into his well-worn play clothes. When he saw his twelve-year-old brother and six-year-old sister, he saw that they too were wearing little more than rags.

His mother then made a telephone call to his uncle and aunt in Kenya. Although he could not hear the words, she spoke rapidly in an anxious tone that, toward the end of the conversation, switched to one of tearful gratitude.

When she hung up, she turned to her children and, with tears in her eyes, told them that their father was waiting for them in Kenya. They were going to surprise him, she said, and the old tattered clothes they had on were to pose as servants.

That night, Nobutu and his siblings were made to lie down on the floor of their station wagon, and their mother covered them with blankets. Nobutu didn't understand why they had to hide for the entire four-hour trip, but he thought it was fun anyway.

His naivety lasted until they arrived at the border, which was gated and guarded by machine-gun-carrying soldiers of Idi Amin's army. Although Nobutu didn't know at the time, Amin's soldiers had been ordered to stop, arrest or execute those of British colonial connections, certain tribal ethnicities, intellectuals, journalists, and religious leaders, among others. If they showed any mercy, they too would be punished, even put to death.

Nobutu's mother parked their car behind a vacant building two blocks away, then the four of them walked slowly and purposely toward the border gate. Once there, Nobutu's mother handed the guard some papers and, speaking in the Ugandan dialect of Swahili, told him that they were servants going to work in the fields of Joseph Mibursu, who Nobutu knew as his uncle in Kenya. After looking over the papers, the guard nodded and opened the gate over the dirt road leading into the safety of Kenya. But just when all was going well, his younger sister turned to her mother and, in flawless English, asked, "Are we going to meet Daddy soon?"

"Halt!" Nobutu heard the guard shout.

"Run—run fast—your daddy is waiting for you down the road!" his mother cried out.

Nobutu would spend the rest of his life trying to forget what happened next. As he ran alongside his brother, several shots rang out, two whistling right over his head. He turned around just in time to see his mother grab the side of her head and fall over like a fallen tree. His baby sister was also shot, the force of the bullet lifting her off the ground and launching her backward several feet. Terrified, Nobutu and his brother kept running and were soon out of sight of the guards, who did not dare to trespass into Kenya given the animosity of that country's government to Idi Amin's regime.

He and his brother ran for what seemed like miles, stopping only when their legs had turned to rubber. It was only then, as they stood gasping for air, that the full import of what had happened hit them. The gasping turned to sobs as they realized they would never see their beloved mother and sister again. The two eventually continued on and connected with their uncle later that day. From him, they learned more devastating news: their father was not waiting for them in Kenya but was dead as well, murdered by Amin's soldiers back in Kampala. In the coming months and years, the boys' grief would turn to hatred for Idi Amin and his henchmen, as well as a deep distrust of government in general.

Thus began the transition of Nobutu Menga to Nobutu Ingale, the name given to him at the tender age of ten when he joined the Uganda National Liberation Army, a fighting force comprised of exiled Ugandans and Tanzanians.

In just two short years, Nobutu had changed from an innocent eight-year-old boy into a savage revolutionary noted for beheading many of Idi Amin's soldiers and slitting the throats of those captured just to see them bleed out. In honor of his courage and ferocity, the NLA renamed him Nobutu Ingale—or lion, a respected symbol in Ugandan culture.

As his power and status grew within the organization, Nobutu became addicted to violence as a means of solving a problem or obtaining what he wanted. In 1979, he and countless others got their wish when the UNLA successfully deposed Idi Amin. Once the dictator was gone, however, there was little improvement. Instead, Nobutu saw Amin's regime replaced by one corrupt government after another—governments that promised liberty only to embezzle public funds for their own gain, restrict travel and other freedoms, and eventually reinstitute a military-backed dictatorship.

Now fifty years old and hardened by decades of bloodshed and brutality, Nobutu has never gotten over what happened to his family. He has also never given up on his mission to restore Uganda to a democratic nation by whatever means necessary.

CHAPTER 4
Sabbatical

Six weeks before Big Jim's assassination of Richard Rimer and Goliath and one month prior to Nobutu Ingale's execution of Choban, a much quieter, nobler mission is about to begin. Professor Randall Lurie, MD, Ph.D., and Chairman of the Infectious Disease and Tropical Medicine Department at Witwatersrand University, also known as "The Vits," is packing for his sabbatical.

"Professor, are you sure you're not overpacking a bit? I understand bringing the usual camping gear, but do you really need culture plates, portable ovens and test tubes? A portable desk? How are you planning to get all this into the field?"

Lurie turns to Albert Kaplan, his research assistant of the past twelve years, and smiles warmly.

"Don't worry, my dear friend. When I land in Kampala, I'll be met by two men—locals who know the rural areas inside and out. They will take me to the spot where I'm to set up camp. It's close to three villages, so, in addition to studying the tropical fungi required for our research grant, I'll also be able to educate and treat the villagers for malaria. You've heard of the malaria outbreak around Lake Victoria?"

Albert nods. "I have."

"Unusually heavy seasonal rains have created an overflow of the lake, which in turn has created a large breeding ground for the mosquitos that carry malaria."

Albert gestures to one of Professor Lurie's overstuffed bags. "Well, I guess that explains all the eco-friendly insect repellents and bottles of antibiotics."

"Yes, doxycycline and Malarone to prevent malaria and treat the villagers who have already contracted it, and ciprofloxacin for other bacterial diseases. You see, Albert, I can do our research and also help the people of our neighboring country at the same time. At least the ones I can reach in the six months of my sabbatical."

"But I thought sabbaticals were a full year...."

"They used to be, Albert, full-year sabbaticals at full salary. Nowadays, most universities can only afford six-month sabbaticals at half salary, and they grant them only to senior tenured professors." He chuckles. "I guess at age seventy-two, I qualify as 'senior'. nevertheless, I must return to work within six months in order to earn my salary. Meanwhile, I'll be able to keep in touch with the satellite radio you just packed. If you don't hear from me every Wednesday at five p.m., let the university president know. He'll know what to do."

Albert looks at his mentor, concerned by the implication that something could happen to him. "Maybe I should go with you, Dr. Lurie. I can help with all the cultures and the treating of villagers just like I do here."

"Really, Albert, there's no need to worry. I've been doing fieldwork since before you were born. Besides, you have plenty of work to do here."

"I'm not worried about the diseases out there or the animals. I'm certainly not doubting your experience or your preparedness. I'm worried about the rebels, Professor. You read the news; they're trying to overthrow the Ugandan government and are killing everything and everyone in their path. How are you going to protect yourself from them?"

Dr. Lurie laughingly runs a hand through his grey hair. "What would the rebels want from an old man like me? I'll be just fine. Now pack those last boxes containing the spray bottles with disinfectant, and be sure to wash your hands afterward so that the harsh chemicals don't irritate your skin."

Two days later, an eight-seater, twin-engine plane lands on a bumpy grass landing strip just north of Lake Victoria. Professor Lurie, seated in the copilot's chair, nervously turns to look at the rear of the plane, which was cleared of its seats so as to accommodate all of his equipment. He hopes the shaking and bouncing from the landing has not broken any of his precious items.

When he deplanes a few minutes later, he finds Mutumbo and Mawanza, the two Ugandan porters he hired, waiting for him. Both standing six feet tall with lean, muscular frames and identical outfits of khaki shorts, short-sleeved shirts and tan boots with calf-length green socks, they look like the quintessential tour guides featured in African safari catalogs. The shorter, stockier Professor

Lurie is dressed much the same with the exception of the full-length khaki pants that are his preference.

Under his watchful eye and with the occasional, "Be careful, my good men," from the professor, Mutumbo and Mawanza transfer Lurie's equipment from the plane to a Land Rover, then they bid farewell to the pilot and drive off.

Less than an hour later, Professor Lurie is gingerly unpacking his things at the campsite. It is located two miles outside an unnamed rural village and just north of the lake near the town of Jinja. It is also the epicenter of the recent malaria outbreaks. With great relief, he finds his equipment undamaged, and for the first time since boarding the plane, he allows himself to relax and look forward to the challenges, both academic and humanitarian, that he has set for himself over the next several months.

***

At first light, Professor Lurie opens his eyes and stretches on his cot. It was another cool, uneventful night punctuated with the chatter of vervet monkeys in the trees, the unmistakable, ascending whoop, whoop, whoop of hyenas on a night prowl, and the occasional trumpeting of an elephant in the distance. Having spent a month at camp, he has grown accustomed to these sounds and even finds them quite comforting.

He moves over to a table in the corner of the tent where he keeps his toiletries, a pitcher of water and a small basin. He pours water into the basin and splashes it onto his face, washing the last vestiges of sleep from his eyes, then dresses quickly. He has a two-mile trek ahead of him, and he's anxious to get to the village.

So far, the sabbatical has been going even better than he anticipated. In just three weeks, Dr. Lurie halted the outbreak of malaria and treated a few cases of cholera, both with the doxycycline he had brought. He also treated two rare cases of anthrax using his ciprofloxacin. During that time, villagers became used to the sight of the gray-haired white doctor with the three-hundred-sixty-degree brimmed hat and affable smile who came to see them twice each week. Mostly, though, they are drawn to his caring demeanor, something to which they are unaccustomed, and often reward him with gifts of fruit and other foods.

For the most part, Professor Lurie is content and happy to be serving those in need of his medical care as well as slowly advancing his research. Yet, while alone at night in his tent, he has had the occasional feeling of uneasiness. He is unsure as to the cause of his anxiety, though the recent rumors of rebel movement in the area haven't helped. He has even wondered at times if the villagers, as friendly as they seem, might be planning to rob him. Whatever its origins, he has been unable to shake the feeling that something unpleasant is going to happen. Perhaps, he thinks as he runs a comb through his gray beard, he has allowed Albert's fears to get to him. The young research assistant sounded most relieved upon receiving his Wednesday evening calls.

"Poor Albert." The professor chuckles, then grabs his hat and exits the tent. However, before him stands three rifle-bearing African men dressed in camouflage. Lurie gasps in surprise then freezes as two of the men point their rifles at him. The third man steps forward, and Lurie knows from his demeanor that he is the leader.

"Who are you," he says in perfect English, "and what are you doing in Uganda?"

"I—I am Professor Randall Lurie," he stammers then launches into an explanation of his university position much to the boredom of the leader. However, when he relates that he has been treating the local villagers for malaria and has in fact halted a malaria epidemic, the leader's eyes widen with intense interest.

"You treat malaria? You can prevent malaria?"

"Certainly, my good man. That is my profession. I brought enough medicines to treat half of Uganda and then some. You know malaria can cripple you and even kill you if you—"

"That's enough, doctor. You and your medicines will come with us. You'll be the medical arm of the Revolutionary Libertarian Army."

The hairs on the back of Lurie's neck stand up. "But, but, but my work here is not done."

"Yes, it is, doctor. You now work for me."

With that, the leader turns and, in rapid-fire Swahili, barks orders to his two troops who immediately lower their rifles and set about packing up Professor Lurie's belongings. The leader steps forward, encloses the professor's arm in a vise-like grip, and begins leading him to a nearby Land Rover.

His heart beating wildly, Professor Lurie manages to call over his shoulder, "Be sure to bring the spray bottles of disinfectant."

"Don't worry, doctor," the leader says with an icy smile. "My men will bring all your things. They won't disobey me."

"Since I'm your captive and apparently now an army doctor, may I ask who you are?"

"My name is Nobutu Ingale," he says as he deposits Lurie in the passenger seat of the vehicle. "If you're a good doctor and treat my troops, no harm will come to you."

CHAPTER 5
The Deal

Two days after the carnage at Kruger, Jim McCullar awakens from a late afternoon nap in his room at 54 on Bath, a quaint and elegant hotel in the posh Rosebank section of Johannesburg. He sits up in bed and is almost startled to see the nude blonde sleeping by his side.

"Sorry, love," he says as he roughly shakes her arm, "but it's time for you to go."

The woman groans. "C'mon, just a few more minutes."

"I know we've had a wild time…" Jim pauses, unable to recall her name. "But now the party's over, and Big Jim's got some business to tend to. I left you some money on the dresser."

Suddenly wide awake, the woman sits up in bed and gives him a withering look. "I told you, I am not a prostitute!"

"Yeah, yeah, that's what you all say.…"

"Oh, screw you," she says, eliciting a snarky look from Jim. She then jumps off the bed and begins struggling into her clothes. Three minutes later, she is gone.

Jim takes a long, hot shower then dresses in his preferred attire: khaki cargo shorts and shirt, and of course the hat. Strategically pinned up on one side, it is emblematic of the outback. In his belt, he places his three knives, including his favorite nine-inch blade, "The Prime Minister," and a 9mm Glock, then slings an empty beige leather satchel over his left shoulder. Before leaving the room, he goes into the closet and pulls the two rhino horns, wrapped in burlap, from the top shelf and tucks them carefully under his right arm.

At precisely seven p.m., he walks out of the hotel and slides into a waiting black sedan.

"We're going to the Intercontinental Hotel at Tambo Airport," he tells the driver, "but we have to make another stop first."

Fifteen minutes later, the driver pulls up to Canton Supreme, a small restaurant in Chinatown. Jim peels off a thousand-rand note, hands it to the driver, and instructs him to wait with the motor running. He then slides from the car and, with one hand on the Glock, enters through the back door into the kitchen area. The air is warm from the ovens and filled with the aroma of ginger, soy sauce and other oriental spices. A few feet from him, two cooks banter back and forth as they prepare their dishes while several waitresses hurriedly pass through the beaded curtain on their way to the dining room.

Jim assesses the scene for a moment then turns in the other direction and heads down a dimly lit hallway toward another beaded curtain. There, in a small, smoky office behind the curtain, sits Chang Li. He doesn't bother to stand as Jim enters the room; he just snuffs out his cigarette in the overflowing ashtray and waves the cloud of smoke away from his face.

"I heard you had a big score, my friend," Chang Li says. "Is that it under your arm?"

"It sure is, and it's a beauty." Jim places the burlap packages on the desk and slowly removes the huge primary horn. "I'll bet it goes over twenty-six kilos, don't you think, Chang?"

Chang Li's eyes widen. He has seen many rhino horns in his line of business, but never one this large or as perfectly formed. He reaches over and strains to lift the horn with both hands.

"Oh yes, definitely over twenty-six kilos."

Jim grunts then pulls out the secondary horn and places it on the desk. "And we have this as well."

Chang Li's round face splits into a rare grin. "Excellent."

"Right. Well then, I'll just take my payment and be off."

Without hesitation, Chang Li reaches into the top drawer of his desk and takes out five wrapped blocks of American money, each marked twenty thousand dollars, and places them on the desk.

Jim's eyes narrow. "Now wait a minute, Chang. We agreed to two hundred thousand. Where's the rest?"

"That's all you get. You are a week late with the goods. My distributors lose clients. I lose money."

"Listen, Chang, I don't give a wombat's ass about your distributors or your clients. A deal is a deal."

Jim hears the beaded curtain move and turns to see a tall, heavily muscled man in an impeccable suit at his side.

"Any trouble, boss?" he asks Chang in a steely tone.

"No, Park Song. Mr. McCullar and I were just conducting some business."

"Don't give me that bullshit, Chang," Jim says with his eyes at Park. "We agreed on two hundred."

Park moves even closer to Jim so that the two are nearly touching. Jim holds the bodyguard's stare for a moment to show he is unfazed by the threat, then turns to Chang and growls, "A deal is a deal, mate."

Chang begins to reply, "Take it or leave it," but before he can get the words out, blood splatter hits his right cheek and covers his glasses. Momentarily blinded by the dark red globs, he doesn't see Park Song's near-decapitated body come crashing down on his desk before slipping to the floor with a sickening thud. Chang takes off his glasses to see the fuzzy image of Jim McCullar calmly stoop down and wipe the blood from his knife onto the dead bodyguard's clothing. He then re-sheathes the "Prime Minister" to meet Chang's horrified stare.

"Now, what were you saying about my fee?"

"Okay, okay," Chang stammers, "whatever you want. Just give me a minute." He runs a hand over his glasses in an attempt to wipe the blood away but succeeds only in smearing it more.

"Now, Chang."

Chang gives two quick nods then swivels around to the safe behind his chair and, with shaking hands, begins fumbling with the lock. After several tries, he finally gets it open, then empties it and places everything on his desk. "Here, take it. Take it all. Just leave, okay?"

McCullar makes a clucking sound with his tongue. "Well, I see you've been holding out on old Big Jim McCullar. That's quite a tidy sum you have there."

"Yes, take it. Just don't kill me. Go! Go!"

"No, Chang, not everything," he says magnanimously. "I'll take my two hundred K and another hundred because you tried to cheat me, but not a penny more. No one can say Big Jim isn't an honest man."

Jim calmly places fifteen banded blocks of the cash into his satchel and closes the latch. Before turning to leave, he tips his hat to the still quivering Chinese man. "Pleasure doing business with you, mate."

CHAPTER 6
The Potion

Promptly at three the next afternoon, Chang Li arrives at the door of his warehouse just two blocks up the street from his restaurant. He has managed to push the carnage of the previous night to the back of his mind thanks to several strong drinks and the anticipation of huge profits he will reap from the sale of the rhino horns in the trunk of his car.

He is greeted by Graphite Persus, the shop foreman and one of Chang's most trusted employees. Graphite belongs to the peaceful Shangaan tribe that separated from the warlike Zulu tribe more than a century ago, a lineage he honors with the tattoo on his left upper arm and the distinctive gold leopard necklace. A well-trained machinist and skilled in factory procedures, his leadership has maintained order and productivity within the warehouse, now converted into a lab of sorts.

"Did you get the big horn, boss?"

"I sure did. It's in the trunk. Bring it in for me, will you, Graphite? It's too heavy for me."

Persus opens the trunk of Chang Li's car and is immediately impressed with the size and shape of the two horns in front of him. He gingerly picks them up and carries them into the main lab area as if he were holding a fragile piece of china. As he sets them down on a table, he is joined by six of his fellow workers, all of whom look at the horns in awe. As native South Africans, they recognize the unusually large size of the primary horn and admire its perfect form. Some feel a fleeting sadness for the loss of an animal their culture has long admired and respected; however, any feelings of remorse soon give way to the practical realization of the money that will come from it—money they desperately need to sustain themselves and each of their several wives.

"Take good care of them," Chang says. "Use both horns, and gather up every bit of the powder you grind out of them." Chang shudders as the vision of Park's bloody body flashes through his mind. "They were very costly."

"No 'hello' for me, Chang?"

Chang Li turns in the direction of the familiar voice to Rob Malmo, Vice President of International Marketing for Apollo Drug Company, emerging from Chang's warehouse office. The forty-something American is smartly dressed as usual in a black Armani suit, white shirt, and a black tie.

"I do say 'hello,' now that I see you, old friend. You been here long?"

"Only fifteen minutes and two cups of coffee. I see you won the grand prize this time."

"Yes, over twenty-six kilos for the big one, and five kilos for the little one. I think they'll easily break the Hong

Kong-Beijing-Bangkok market price record of 1.2 million US."

"Congratulations, Chang, and with our new booster, your distributors will knock the competition out of the picture."

Chang looks at him, perplexed. "New booster? Why a new booster? The one you've been giving us is doing fine. All my distributors report much better and longer-lasting power than the powdered horn alone, or anything our competitors have."

"Relax, my friend," Malmo chuckles. "As we say in the marketing game, this powder is 'new and improved,' guaranteed to make any guy feel like a porn star and last just as long."

"You've sold me already." Chang laughs as Malmo leads him and Graphite to the back of the warehouse where his shipment is stored.

"There it is, Chang—five crates, each containing a thousand vials, ready to house your powdered horn. Let me show you two how to do it. First, the area must be sterile, so be sure your workers scrub up and wear masks, gloves, and gowns, just like in an operating room. Take the rubber stopper off the vial, and add one ounce of powdered horn to our booster powder, which is already in each vial. Then you're going to put the stopper back on and mix the two powders like this." Malmo takes one of the three-inch-long vials, the size and shape of a chemistry lab test tube, lengthwise between his thumb and middle finger and turns it up and down like an hourglass. "You're going to do this ten times."

"Ten times," Graphite repeats, "got it."

"We put a light electrical charge on our booster powder," Malmo continues, "so the two ingredients will adhere to the keratin of the rhino horn. No refrigeration is necessary. You can then ship these to all your Asian, US and European contacts." Malmo flashes them a smile. "It will be, as we say in the US pharmaceutical industry, a blockbuster drug."

***

While Chang Li and Rob Malmo are going over the mixing technique, Jim McCullar is awakening after another all-nighter, this time in the honeymoon suite at the Airport Intercontinental Hotel. As he blinks the sleep out of his eyes, he turns to see Blessing, a young black woman with smooth, bronze skin and a tall, slender physique, naked and sleeping soundly at the far end of the oversized bed. He then notices a warm weight on his chest and realizes it's Brenda, a white South African with strawberry blond hair and a 38-D cup. The "B and B Girls," as he affectionately calls them, are his favorite escorts, and he makes it a point to book them every time he passes through Johannesburg. The room is strewn with half-empty champagne bottles and, of course, Jim's favorite—Crown Royal blended whiskey. There are no drugs to be found as Jim forbids his girls to bring or use them. He wants a "natural experience."

Feeling him stir, Brenda begins to massage his chest.

"No time for that, love," he says groggily. "I have to get going. Gotta be in Uganda by tonight."

Brenda says nothing; she just smiles wickedly at him and continues rubbing his chest.

"Then again," Jim says with a resigned tone, "there's always time for one more...."

With that, he quickly turns Brenda around and enters her from behind. Amidst her giggles of acceptance and moans of pleasure, Jim pumps her hard for a full five minutes, bringing them both to orgasm and proving to himself once again that, whether it is in the jungle or the bedroom, his performance is unparalleled.

CHAPTER 7
The So-Called Vacation – Part 1

"Robert, what do you think of this? It would look great on that bare wall in my office."

Dr. Robert Merriweather looks at the painting his fiancée, Heather Bellaire, is pointing to. After a quick appraisal, he nods his approval then watches as she begins the bargaining process with the proprietor of the cubicle, one of the many in the African Crafts Market adjacent to the 54 on Bath Hotel. A few minutes later, she hands him the painting with a satisfied smile and asks him to carry it so that she can continue shopping unencumbered.

Though Robert has been to the market many times before, being there with Heather for the first time has allowed him to see it with new eyes. She marveled at the market's entrance, an attractive archway lined on either side with metal mesh and very lifelike replicas of Africa's Big Five. And her eyes grew wide when she saw the sea of cubicles in the ten-thousand-square-foot space, each containing various curios, carvings, paintings, and kitchen wares, all sold by the artisans who created them.

The two had arrived in Johannesburg three days earlier, jet-lagged and exhausted. Robert's journey was particularly grueling as he first had to fly from Miami to New York to meet Heather, then the two of them boarded the South African Airways jet for the sixteen-hour flight. They spent that first day resting and the next two taking in the local sights.

As they strolled through Nelson Mandela's house and toured the diamond mines and the archeologic sites at Stroheim, where the earliest known pre-human hominid fossils could be seen, Robert couldn't help but think of the times he and his ex-wife Veronica visited these treasures while in Joburg, their stop-off point before embarking on photographic safaris into the South African bush. Trips like this were the favorite of Veronica, who preferred nature explorations, particularly those involving animals, over luxury cruises or stuffy concerts in crowded major cities. She especially loved the African Crafts Market, which to her represented a throwback to earlier times and a distinct contrast to the adjacent mall filled with high-end jewelry, clothing stores, and boutiques. Robert recalls how she never tired of hearing the come-ons from proprietors claiming their wares were more beautiful than any other in the market, her delight when she found a rare treasure amidst the mass-produced curios, and her skill at bargaining, something for which he had little patience. Suddenly, he finds himself filled with a rare and rather uncomfortable feeling of nostalgia.

"Oh, the boys would love these!" Heather exclaims, bringing Robert back to the present. He looks over to see her clutching two elephants carved from wood and nods absently.

Robert forces the memories of his ex from his mind and dutifully follows Heather as she completes the purchase then moves on to the next cubicle and begins scrutinizing each item.

Humans have not really evolved very much from their cave-dwelling ancestors, he muses. They emigrated from Africa and into Europe some three hundred thousand years ago to eventually displace the resident Neanderthals. Yet here we are today, the same hunter-gatherers as they were.

Warming to his subject, he thinks about cavemen, hunters whose single-minded purpose was to kill game for food. They would seek out their prey, single out one target, and go after it. Though today's men don't have to look further than the fridge for a meal, they do approach life in the same way as their ancestors. They know what they want, be it a fishing lure, a briefcase, or a car, and go after it.

Cavewomen, on the other hand, were the gatherers, dutifully collecting edible fruits, berries, firewood and even medicinal plants. They had to carefully select each one and choose the tastier ones, the nonpoisonous ones, and the ones experience told them would treat an ailment. They had to be selective. They had to look over each item slowly and carefully—a trait that, evidenced by the way Heather was pouring over the wares, seemed to be present today.

Yes, men are still men, and women are still women, he thinks. *Well, except for transgender and nonbinary individuals ... still can't figure those out* he continues to muse. Robert chuckles at his politically incorrect thought and follows Heather to yet another cubicle.

After a few more moments of observing his fiancée in her native habitat, Robert admits to himself that he is officially bored. Not wanting to cut Heather's fun short, he wanders down another aisle in search of something that sparks his interest. Around him, people from all parts of the world are milling about, laughing, bargaining, and enjoying time with family and friends.

Suddenly, Robert notices a man that, even among the blend of cultures, races and walks of life, seems oddly out of place. At first, Robert thinks the man—white, in his mid-thirties and wearing cutoff jeans, a "Guns N' Roses" T-shirt, and tattered sneakers—stands out because he is dressed differently than the other tourists. But no, that's not it. The man doesn't just look different, he is acting different. For as he meanders about the aisles, he is not looking at the items in the cubicles but at other people, particularly women.

All traces of boredom gone, Robert follows him at a distance. The man appears to be trailing a young brunette as she goes from one cubicle to another. Each time, he stops pretending to look at some items then moves on just after she does. He looks like he's about to speak with her when suddenly another man walks up and puts an arm around her shoulders. They walk away together, leaving the odd man standing there alone. He begins wandering aimlessly again, only to repeat the same pattern with another young woman until she too is joined by her boyfriend or husband.

A growing concern tugs at Robert's mind, and he remembers that Heather is somewhere alone in the market. Glancing around, he catches a glimpse of her at a cubicle at the end of an aisle, far removed from his suspected stalker. Relieved, Robert turns back to the man and, with a start, realizes he is now focused on a girl about ten years old.

I've been watching too much "Investigative Discovery," he tells himself and is about to return to Heather when he sees the man pull out his phone and make a quick call. A moment later, he is bending down to talk to the girl.

Robert realizes that they—the stalker and himself—have made a loop of the market and are back near the entrance. He looks past the arch and notices a green Toyota parked out front, an unusual sight in an area almost exclusively populated by pedestrians. The driver, also a white, scruffy-looking man, is gripping the wheel as he is seen to be glancing nervously about. Try as he might, Robert cannot shake the feeling that the two men are connected. He also feels quite certain that a child abduction is about to unfold. He automatically scans the area for a security guard then recalls that he has never seen such a person in the market.

What if I'm imaging things? he asks himself. *What if the man is the girl's father or an uncle?* Yet, even as he is doubting his instincts, he finds himself moving toward the entrance, almost as if taking up his post.

Any hesitation quickly vanishes when the stalker points to some stuffed animals a few feet away from where Robert is standing. The girl smiles, then the two start walking toward the animals. Suddenly, he claps a hand over her mouth, lifts her up, and starts running the short distance to the entrance and, presumably, the waiting car. He has nearly made it when Robert puts Heather's painting down and steps forward, throwing a shoulder into him and knocking both the man and the girl he is carrying into the stuffed animal stand. Released from the would-be abductor's grasp, the girl bursts into tears and rushes back into the market. Robert pounces on the man, pinning him to the ground face down.

Within seconds, security guards and police from the adjacent mall rush to the scene and, thinking Robert and the man are fighting, attempt to separate them.

"He tried to kidnap a girl," Robert gasps. "I saw the whole thing."

As the police move to handcuff the would-be kidnapper, Robert glanced in the direction of the suspicious Toyota only to find it gone. He rushes past the entrance and sees that the driver has pulled away from the curb and is now blocked by a large number of pedestrians crossing in front of him. Robert quickly commits the license plate numbers to memory then returns to the police officers to give them the information.

He soon finds himself at the center of a growing crowd of curious onlookers. As one officer escorts the prisoner from the premises, another begins asking Robert questions about the failed abduction. As he tells the story of how he observed the man following various women, Robert notes the dubious expression on the officer's face.

"Are you some sort of detective, sir?"

"No," Robert says, beginning to grow angry at the cop's attitude, "I am Dr.—"

Just then, he hears a voice softly say, "That's the man."

Robert looks down and sees the young girl the man tried to abduct. Her blonde hair is mussed, and her eyes are red from crying. Beside her is a woman in her late thirties. The resemblance between the two is unmistakable, and Robert knows this must be her mother.

"Officer, this man saved my daughter from being kidnapped," she says, her voice breaking. "He's a hero." She turns to Robert. "I don't know how I can ever repay you for saving my Angela."

"All I did was bump into the guy," Robert says, uncomfortable with the word "hero". To his dismay, several in the crowd begin clapping and cheering. He offers them a sheepish smile and says, "I'm just glad it worked out okay."

Suddenly, he feels Angela's arms around him.

"Thank you for saving me, mister!"

"Why you're welcome, Angela," Robert says awkwardly. "You know what? The guy who tried to take you away is going to jail, and his accomplice who was going to drive you away will be caught as well because we got his license plate number. I guess you and I make a good team for catching crooks, don't we?"

Angela smiles, then, with another parting thank you, her relieved mother begins leading her away.

"You're a hero to me," he hears Heather say and turns to find her standing by his side, her eyes welling, "and you always will be." Suddenly, her face splits into a grin. "Can I count on the rest of our vacation being this exciting? After all, you do seem to invite adventure wherever you go."

Robert chuckles. "I'm not making any promises, but perhaps on the safari at Simbambili. It means 'two lions.'"

Heather squeezes his hand. "Well, adventurous or not, it'll be nice just to be together away from our work."

"Amen to that," concludes Robert.

Chapter 8
The So-Called Vacation – Part 2

The following morning, Robert and Heather are picked up from the 54 on Bath Hotel by Wildlife Safari's transport and taken to the domestic terminal at Tambo International Airport. As the vehicle passes by homes and small businesses surrounded by barbed wire fencing, Robert is thankful that his friends at Karell African Vacations have organized his entire trip. Despite being a thriving city and considered the jewel of Africa, Johannesburg is a crime-ridden and dangerous place, as attested to by yesterday's abduction attempt.

At the airport, they are greeted and met by another wildlife safari host and guided through security to the appropriate gate for the two-hour flight to the airfield at Nelspruit, just west of Krueger National Park.

"This is wonderful," Heather says as they settle into their seats on the forty-seater plane. "Thank you for arranging everything."

Robert kisses her on the cheek. "It's my pleasure, my dear."

Just then, he feels a tap on his shoulder. He turns around

to find himself face to face with the little girl he rescued at the market.

"Angela! Are you going on a safari too?"

"We are!" She peers at him curiously. "I heard you tell the cop you're a doctor. Is that right?"

"Yes, I'm a surgeon. I fix messed up jaws and faces and remove cancers too."

"I want to be a doctor when I grow up."

"That's wonderful, my dear. The world can always use more good doctors." He glances around. "Where is your mom?"

"She's sitting a few rows back. We're meeting my dad at Simbambili. He's coming from a business trip."

Heather gestures to two empty seats across the aisle. "Why don't you and your mom move next to us?"

Angela gives them an excited nod, and a few minutes later, the four of them are chatting amiably. Robert and Heather learn that Kimberly, Angela's mom, and her husband are from Milwaukee, Wisconsin but have lived in Johannesburg for the past two years due to his work duties.

"He's in marketing," she explains, "and covers all of Africa and India, which keeps him away for long periods."

Before Robert can ask her what company he works for, the pilot announces their descent into Nelspruit.

Seated at the window, Heather notices the somewhat dry landscape with bush, a few trees, and crisscrossing dirt roads. She spots a water hole as the plane descends further and excitedly announces, "Hey, there are hippos in the water and one out on the banks."

Robert gives her a knowing smile. "This is just the beginning. Wait till our first game drive this afternoon."

The plane buzzes the airstrip to be sure no animals, particularly elephants, are on or about to cross the runway; then, once given the all-clear, circles around to land.

The small airport at Nelspruit is mostly a jumping-off point for several safari camps. After getting off the plane, the travelers are met by a bush pilot who will fly them a short distance to a small grass landing strip within the private game reserve shared by several of these camps.

"Daddy!" Angela cries out.

Robert and Heather turn to see a handsome, dark-haired man rushing toward them.

"Hey, honey." He hugs Angela then kisses Kimberly on the cheek. "I thought I was going to miss my flight from Maun in Botswana."

Before Kimberly can introduce them to her husband, a wildlife host ushers them to the twin-engine, eight-seater aircraft that will take them on the next leg of their journey.

Fifteen minutes later, the bush pilot buzzes the runway at Simbambili, this time to scatter a small herd of zebra grazing on the south end, then smoothly takes the plane down. This time, the travelers are met by Darryl Sterling, the ranger, and White, the tracker, who gather up their luggage into a Land Rover and head off on dirt roads leading to the main camp. Like all safari first-timers, Heather's jaw drops in astonishment at the sight of the tracker sitting on a small chair attached to the left side grill plate, exposed to the wildlife including lions and leopards.

On the way, they learn that Darryl is an expert in African wildlife and possesses a wealth of knowledge about the animals, seasons, terrain, trees and other plant life. White, a native Shangann African, is considered the camp's best tracker.

Arriving at the main camp, the five are met by the manager and staff with a fruit drink and a cooling towel. After the manager signs everyone in and goes over the camp rules, the staff takes their luggage to their suites. It is then that Kimberly's husband steps toward Robert with a warm smile and an extended hand.

"Hi, I'm Robert Malmo. My wife told me how you saved my daughter yesterday from some pervert. I can't thank you enough. I hope I can do something for you in return."

"Nice to meet you, Robert. I'm Bob Merriweather from Miami. And that lovely lady," he gestures to Heather, who is looking out the veranda at the water hole, "is my fiancée, Heather."

Malmo gives Merriweather a curious stare. "Angela said you're a doctor. Are you by any chance the Dr. Robert

Merriweather who was the expert witness against Apollo and North Star drug companies two years ago in the trials over the cis-phosphorus complications?"

"Why yes. How do you know about that?"

"Well, I work for Apollo as their International Marketing Director. The cis-phosphorus cases were just coming to the courts when I joined Apollo. I can tell you that yours is the most single hated name in our company."

Robert laughs. "I can assure you the ill will is mutual. But let's not let that unpleasantness affect our vacations. I've been to Simbambili three times before. It's one of my favorite places, and I hope it'll become a favorite of Heather's as well. I'm sure your wife and little Angela will find it fascinating and a great learning experience. Let's just enjoy the days ahead and each other."

"You've got a deal, Dr. Merriweather," Malmo says with a grin. "I owe you at least that much."

Robert waves his words away. "Say, why don't I call you Bob M-1 and you can call me Bob M-2?"

Malmo laughs. "Great idea, Dr. Merr—I mean Bob M-2."

They walk over to the veranda, where Heather, Kimberly and Angela are watching a small herd of elephants cavorting at the watering hole, drinking, trumpeting, and spraying the cooling water over their backs.

"Incredible," Heather says, slipping an arm around Robert's waist. "If it's all I saw here, I'd leave happy."

Robert smiles at her. "Just you wait."

The first day at Simbambili is a relaxed schedule of lunch followed by some time to rest until it's time to get ready for the evening game drive at five o'clock. This allows them to journey for two hours in daylight then make the return after sunset so they can see the nocturnal animals and view the spectacular Southern Cross constellation in a star-filled sky. The rest of the trip will be the perfect blend of structure and downtime so guests can get the wildlife experience and still have time for R&R. Each morning, they will rise at five-thirty and be escorted to the main lodge by their rifle-carrying ranger. There, they can have a scone or muffin, coffee or tea before heading out on the morning game drive.

When the drive concludes at about nine a.m., everyone will return to camp for a lavish breakfast followed by a few hours of free time. Then it's back to the lodge for a huge lunch, though many guests are still too full from breakfast to eat much. Between the hours of one and five, they will have the opportunity to visit the library, get a massage, use the workout room, or just gaze out the window at the various animals as they drink from the watering hole.

This is referred to as the stationary game drive. Although, for Dr. Merriweather, the real fun is going on a bushwalk with the always armed and incredibly knowledgeable rangers to learn about game-tracking, analysis of animal droppings known as scat, as well as the insects, lizards, and plant life. It is something he never tires of no matter how many trips he has taken to Simbambili.

He planned this rich experience of the African bush to

introduce Heather to what he enjoys most, but now he finds himself questioning that decision. She enjoyed looking out at the watering hole, but would she truly like such an outdoorsy vacation? He has always thought of her as more of a lay on the beach with a mai tai type of person. Had he been selfish?

Robert puts these second thoughts aside as he and Heather enter their suite with its direct view of the watering hole and a dry creek bed that several game animals, leopards in particular, seek out to lie in the cool sand. Inside, a king-sized bed with beautiful mosquito netting overlying it sits in the center. In an adjacent room, they find a marbled shower and a bathtub along with a plethora of bottles of soaps and lotions scented with African fragrances. For the more adventurous guest, there is an outside shower as well as a six-by-six-foot "plunge pool" in the middle of the deck. Cushioned lounge chairs provide the perfect spot to rest after a dip or take in the sunset.

Very early the following morning, Robert and Heather slip out of bed and quickly dress in layered, comfortable clothes. It is August, the height of the winter in South Africa, so they can expect the temperature to reach only fifty-five degrees or so. After a quick muffin and coffee, they follow Ranger Darryl and Tracker White to the tiered Range Rover. Darryl slides behind the steering wheel, which is on the right side consistent with British driving rules, while White sits on the left side of the grill plate so he can keep an eye peeled for animals or their fresh tracks on the dirt road ahead.

As the Malmos go to take their seats on the top tier of the vehicle, Angela announces that she would rather sit next to Dr. Merriweather. Rather moved, Robert pats the seat beside him. He has taken a genuine liking to the girl, and he is also hoping their friendship will show Heather that there is more to him than the authoritative workaholic she has come to know.

It doesn't take long before they come upon a herd of impala, often called the "McDonald's of the bush" because of the M-shaped patch on their rumps and because they frequently fall prey to leopards, hyenas, wild dogs, and the occasional lion.

Next, they come upon a herd of zebra and several kudu, the large, spiral-horned antelope species. Just then, White raises his hand for Darryl to stop the vehicle.

"A full-grown female leopard," White announces as he gestures to some tracks crossing the dirt road. "About fifteen minutes ago, heading west. Probably Monju."

Darryl explains that they have known Monju since she was a cub. Now almost four years old, she has two cubs of her own. He then takes off into the bush, crashing over small shrubs and trees while White simultaneously deflects branches away from the seated passengers and keeps his eye on the broken twigs and matted grass that identifies the tracks of the leopard.

Five minutes later, they come upon Monju and her six-week-old cubs under the overhang of a low bush. The passengers watch in delight as the cubs nurse, frolic together, then return to their mother for a second helping before falling asleep. Darryl calls in Monju's location so other guests can stop and see her little family.

Halfway through the morning game drive, Darryl again stops the vehicle and invites Robert, Heather, and the Malmos to exit the Land Rover. As they stretch their legs, the two rangers hook up an extension to the grill plate that serves as a serving platform. Within minutes, they have prepared a small feast of biscuits, dried fruits and biltong, a form of beef jerky, along with tea, coffee and hot chocolate. As they eat, the five talk about the amazing sights they have seen thus far, and all agree that seeing Monju and her cubs is the highlight.

"It's amazing that we got so close without scaring her off," Heather says. "It was like we were invisible."

"And the cubs were so cute," Angela gushes, "like the kitties in the pet store."

Robert Merriweather explains that, while they share some characteristics with their domesticated cousins, they will grow up to be fierce hunters. "You don't want to pet them," he admonishes with a smile, "especially when their mother is around."

After the snack, they pile back into the Land Rover to continue the game drive and soon come upon a herd of over three hundred massive Cape buffalo. This is followed by a visit to a large pool in which about twenty hippos could be seen with their heads out of the water, shaking their ears clear of the ubiquitous hippo flies, then a viewing of several crocodiles lying motionless on the bank. They spend several minutes studying the reptiles before a marabou stork flying overhead spooks all of them into the water. As the others chatter in amazement about what they have seen, Robert makes mental notes of the questions he will ask Darryl when they do their bushwalk later in their stay.

Promptly at 9:00 a.m., they are back at the camp, starving and ready to dive into the sumptuous breakfast already laid out for them.

After breakfast, Robert and Heather spend most of their free time alone on the veranda, sipping South African wine and viewing the numerous animals that saunter up to the watering hole for a drink.

Before they know it, Robert, Heather, and the Malmos are meeting up again for the evening game drive, which will take them in the opposite direction from the one this morning.

As they climb into the Land Rover, Darryl informs the crew that the resident pride of lions are enjoying a feast after a successful hunt last night. The travelers, including young Angela, are surprised to find themselves excited at the thought of seeing lions gorging themselves on a recently killed animal.

Indeed, the scene when the Land Rover pulls up to the pride is one of raw nature that might sound repulsive in the abstract but is utterly mesmerizing when viewed in person. On some primal level, each of them understands that the blood, the growling and infighting between the lions, and the ripping of skin and flesh—even the eerie presence of vultures waiting for leftovers—is just part of nature. In this place, the only role for humans is that of a neutral observer.

Darryl informs them that the two males in the center of the kill are brothers who took over the pride three years ago. Now age seven, they are in their prime and protect the six lionesses and their twelve cubs. They have been named Hercules and Atlas due to their massive size and strength.

After leaving the lions, they are treated to a close-up view of two white rhinos, a troop of baboons, and a male leopard, which is found only because White points out a faint smell similar to popcorn in the air. The smell of male leopards and even some females closely resembles that of popcorn and is frequently used by trackers to locate this solitary and elusive cat. As the day comes to a close, the Land Rover stops for a wine and cheese repast around the grill plate shelf—a salute to the setting sun referred to as a sundowner.

"To the animals of the African bush," Robert says as he raises his glass of Amarula, a traditional African drink.

"Here, here," the others reply, earning grins from Darryl and White.

Robert takes in Heather's shining eyes and knows that she too has fallen in love with the African bush, much as Veronica had many years ago. A memory from his and Veronica's first trip together rises unbidden to his mind, bringing with it an odd feeling of guilt mixed with sadness. He shakes his head as if to rid himself of the thought, then feels Heather's hand on his.

"Everything okay, Robert?" she asks.

"Yes, my dear, everything is just fine."

***

On their last night at Simbambili, Robert and Heather arrive at the lodge for dinner only to be greeted not by the Malmos but by smiling staff members.

"Follow us," they say to the surprised couple, who soon find themselves climbing up a rope ladder to the top level of the resort. Somehow, the staff learned of their engagement and arranged a romantic "tree house" dinner under soft lantern lights and a thatched roof. As they sit down to the impeccably prepared meal laid out before them, they hear the nighttime symphony of hyena calls mingled with gentle clucking sounds of yellow and red-billed hornbill birds, chirping crickets and croaking tree frogs.

"What could be more romantic," Robert asks, "than a candlelit dinner under the moonlight?"

"A candlelit dinner under the moonlight with hyenas." Heather laughs gaily and raises her wineglass to his.

After making sure they have everything they need, the staff leaves them to enjoy the meal. Robert is just about to dip his spoon into his soup when a moth beats him to it, diving headlong into the bowl. Within seconds, several moths attracted by the lanterns flutter around Heather's head, with some landing in her wine and her hair. Robert tries to shoo the moths away from her, an attempt at chivalry that results in Heather's wineglass spilling over onto her lap. In the meantime, more and more moths collect around each source of light until they appear like a swarm of locusts. Within minutes, the besieged couple are climbing back down the rope ladder, clutching the remaining morsels of their dinner that is now topped with fluttering moths. Once back in the safety of their suite, they take in each other's food-stained clothes, disheveled hair, and near-empty plates, and burst out laughing.

They are still chuckling when, several minutes later, they are seated across from each other just inside the sliding glass door of their suite leading to the deck.

"Well, so much for a romantic final night in the African Bush," Robert says as he sips from a fresh glass of wine.

"I'll say," Heather says, then, with a mischievous look in her eyes, she picks up her glass and slips out onto the deck.

Robert watches her, enchanted, as she seductively drops her clothes around her feet. He stands up to join her but first stops by the bathroom to pick up two large, fluffy bath towels before stepping onto the deck. There, with a mischievous smile of his own, he turns on the outside shower. As he does, he hears a splash and an immediate "Yeow-oh-oh-oh, its freeeee-zing."

He had a feeling Heather didn't realize the unheated plunge pool is seven feet deep and cold in August. Laughing, he strips off his clothes and jumps right in, enjoying the invigorating bite of the cold on his skin. Then, with his hair slicked back and body covered in goosebumps, he bounds off the bottom to wrap an arm around the shivering Heather. With the other arm, he grips onto the pool's edge.

"Why didn't you tell me the pool is so cold and so deep?" she asks.

Robert grins. "I thought it would be fun to watch you discover it on your own."

"You creep!" Heather exclaims, chuckling.

"Oh, and I hope you're not counting on sex in the pool," Robert adds. "You know what cold water does to a man's manhood.

Heather looks at him with feigned incredulity. "Are you telling me you can't 'rise above' the situation?"

They burst out laughing, then Robert nods toward the running outside shower. "Sure, with a little help I can."

He then helps Heather out of the cold plunge pool, and the two rush over to stand under the hot, steaming spray.

The next morning, their last before returning to Johannesburg, begins as all the others. They head out the circular driveway and down the ravine, onto the dry riverbed. During the dry season, the sand is cooler than the midday air, and it is a place to find a relaxing leopard, pride of lions, or even a herd of elephants feasting on the lush foliage and young tree branches.

To their delight, they come across a pack of African wild dogs, twenty in all including eight puppies. Known as the most efficient hunters in all of Africa, these "painted wolves" as they are called have a successful kill rate of seventy-five percent, which is much better than the leopard at forty percent and the lion at thirty-five percent.

This is attributed to their sleek, trim body style, which gives them exceptional stamina, and a dark brown and tan coat that provides them with excellent camouflage. Their tactic is to hunt as a coordinated pack, which keeps their prey running to the point of exhaustion. From there, it is an easy kill.

Darryl and White, as well as their five passengers, are delighted to see the excitement and yelping of the puppies as the adults periodically return from a kill, probably close by, to regurgitate meat from their stomachs for them. All are amazed to see the puppies get excited minutes before an adult returns to feed them and wonder how these youngsters know a meal is coming. For the next forty-five minutes, they watch the pups compete and fight for every scrap—real-life evidence of the phrases "it's a dog-eat-dog world" and "survival of the fittest."

Leaving the pack of wild dogs, Darryl deftly shifts the gears of the Land Rover to climb over the steep, rock-strewn bank of the sandy bed and back onto a level road.

They are cruising along the road for ten minutes when Angela suddenly shouts, "Lions!" and points to the right. The others turn to see two barely visible maned heads in the tall grass. Grinning proudly that she was the first one to notice them, she asks, "Can we go over to see them up close like the other day?"

Darryl turns the vehicle onto the soft, tall grass field and slowly approaches the lions. As they get close, all are horrified to see the lions feasting not on animals but two human carcasses! One victim is already half-eaten, with the bigger of the lions tearing at what is left of his abdomen. The second lion is lying next to his victim, who has a large portion of each leg missing. The scene becomes even more gruesome when the larger lion turns to look at them, his facial fur stained by the victim's blood.

As Kimberly places her hands over Angela's eyes, Darryl and White jump from the Land Rover with rifles in hand. Dr. Merriweather and Robert Malmo follow cautiously behind them over the protestations of Heather and Kimberly. They all watch, mesmerized, as each ranger fires two shots into the air and starts walking straight at the two lions.

As they hoped, the noise of the rifle shots—and the lions' natural fear of a bipedal animal—results in each lion giving up his kill and running away. They give a backward glance at the humans then face forward and run even faster after two more shots are fired into the air above them.

Once the lions are gone, the two Roberts rush to the side of each victim. Dr. Merriweather takes the pulse of the less-eaten victim in the faint hope for a sign of life, but one touch of the cold skin tells him the man has been dead for some time. For a long moment, Robert Malmo stares in shock at the carnage and the flies buzzing about the wounds then announces weakly that he is returning to the Land Rover.

Meanwhile, Darryl is calmly assessing the scene. The dead men are native black Africans in their mid-thirties and dressed in gray T-shirts, worn brown shorts, and black sneakers. He announces that they are the poachers some of the rangers have caught glimpses of during the evening game drives.

"We've been trying to catch them for weeks," Darryl says, his voice void of sympathy. "We suspect that they have a stash of rifles somewhere in the bush for killing rhinos. See, look over there! It's their walkie-talkie. They must've walked right into an ambush by those two lions last night or, more likely, early this morning. There are no signs of them trying to run away."

Just then, White breaks in. "Darryl, human footprints off to the east. There were three of them."

As White kneels down to examine the footprint, he is joined by Dr. Merriweather, who points out small droplets of blood. White nods, then they follow the footprints, which continue through the two-foot-high grass. While White moves forward, slowly taking in each angle of the trampled grass and the degree of blood on it, Dr. Merriweather looks up and scans in the direction of the trampled grass trail.

"White, Darryl! There he is, in the tree!"

All three rush to a third, similarly dressed African man draped over the branch of a large Marula tree about eight feet off the ground. He appears to be unconscious or perhaps even dead. Darryl takes a quick look back at the kill site and the Land Rover to make sure the lions haven't returned. Then, satisfied that Robert Malmo and his family are safe in the vehicle, he helps White and Dr. Merriweather pull the third victim from his perch.

Dr. Merriweather quickly grabs the man's wrist and, unable to find a radial pulse, moves his hand to the carotid artery and places his right ear over the mouth.

"He's alive, but barely," he announces. "He has a carotid pulse that is weak and slow. He is also breathing." He turns to look at the rangers. "We need to get this man back to camp fast. Do you have an emergency kit there?"

"Yes," Darryl replies, "the same ones they have on international airline flights."

Dr. Merriweather is familiar with the one on American Airlines, having used it on three separate occasions. In fact, he has often said that the American Airlines kits are better stocked than the ones in his own hospital back in Miami.

"Good, we need to get some fluids into him right away. I'll try to start an IV at camp, but he'll really need blood. Let's get him into the Land Rover right now."

The three carefully lift the comatose victim off the ground and carry him to the vehicle, then Robert climbs in beside him. As they head back to camp, he continues to bark out orders as if he is running a code blue emergency in his hospital.

"Heather, open your water bottle, and soak this handkerchief. Place it above the man's mouth. Dripping water on the back of his tongue and throat muscles will trigger his swallowing reflex. Keep dripping it slowly for the entire trip to camp. He needs every drop of fluid. Only stop if he starts to choke or cough, okay?"

"Got it, Bob," Heather says breathlessly.

"Darryl, call ahead to Nelspruit or Hoedspruit or even Joburg air rescue. We need them to bring eight units of

O-negative blood and a rescue team. If it's by helicopter, they should come directly to the camp. If they come by airplane, we'll meet them at your airstrip."

Darryl relays the necessary information to the camp manager while carefully navigating the bumpy roads back to the camp. Dr. Merriweather checks the poacher's pulse continuously while Heather keeps the water dropping to the back of his throat. Along the way, they pass the resident pride of lions sleeping soundly in the shade of a jackalberry tree, making each of the passengers think again about the gruesome scene they have just left. Shortly after, they are met by another Land Rover, this one with camp rangers on their way to pick up the mutilated bodies and spray the area to hopefully reduce the scent of human flesh. No one wants a leopard, hyena, or lion to be aware of the edibility of human prey.

Arriving at the camp, Dr. Merriweather rushes to the emergency kit, which is already open and strewn out on one of the tables on the veranda, while Darryl, White, and the camp manager bring the poacher and lay him down on an adjacent table.

Surveying the well-organized and seemingly never-before-used emergency kit, Dr. Merriweather announces, "Good, there are IV bags and an IV kit as well as all the meds I need. Put several pillows behind his head and back. His veins are all collapsed, so in order to start an IV, I'll need to channel as much blood to his arms as possible." He turns to Malmo. "Bob M-1, do you know how to take blood pressure?"

"Certainly," he replies, looking relieved that he has been

assigned a task that doesn't involve any gore.

As Dr. Merriweather dons a pair of sterile gloves and instructs Malmo and Heather to do the same, he places a rubber tourniquet on the right arm and searches for a vein.

A moment later, Malmo shouts, "Blood pressure sixty over thirty and a pulse of forty-two."

With the loss of blood, low blood pressure and a weak, thready pulse, Dr. Merriweather finds it difficult to find a vein. He tries and misses twice. Knowing the man will die if he cannot fluid resuscitate him now and buy time to receive the transfusion of blood that he really needs, he grabs a scalpel and some sterile gauze.

"M-1, you come here and be my assistant. Heather, you are now a circulating nurse, okay?"

"Sure, I'll do whatever I can."

"Just hand us what we ask for from the kit. I need to do a vein cutdown."

Dr. Merriweather makes a two-inch incision in the right antecubital fossa on the front side of the elbow joint. He notices the minimal oozing of blood from the skin, which is indicative of the poacher's low blood pressure. He also notices the dark color of the blood, indicating its poor oxygenation. A slightly green-looking Robert Malmo retracts the skin as instructed by Dr. Merriweather while the antecubital vein is isolated. Dr. Merriweather then asks Heather for a rubber vein loop to lift up the vein he has just freed up from the surrounding tissue. Heather at first hesitates, as she doesn't know what a rubber vein loop is, but quickly surmises that the thin blue rubber strand that looks like spaghetti must be it. She has guessed right. Dr. Merriweather inserts the rubber loop under the vein and then looks at Malmo.

"M-1, when I cut this vein, blood will come out. Use the gauze to blot the area so I can see the lumen of the vein, and also hand me the IV at the same time. It's all set up."

Within minutes, the makeshift surgical team has executed the transection of the vein and insertion of a fourteen-gauge catheter into the vein. Once in the lumen. Dr. Merriweather tells Heather to open up the valve in the IV line fully. He watches the fluid rapidly transit through the IV drip chamber from the IV bag taped to a nearby lamp post.

As Dr. Merriweather sutures the catheter tightly into the vein and sutures the skin less tightly to allow for swelling, Bob M-1 takes a new blood pressure reading and finds it is still a low sixty over forty. Dr. Merriweather waits for more of the fluid to go in and searches through the emergency drugs in the kit. He prepares a dose of 0.8 milligrams of atropine and dilutes an epinephrine dose from 1:1,000 to 1:10,000, reminding himself that too great a concentration of epinephrine may throw the heart into fibrillation.

He looks up at the IV bag, where 800 milliliters of 1,000 milliliters of normal saline has already gone in. There is only one more liter in the emergency kit. The blood pressure has only improved slightly to seventy over forty. Dr. Merriweather looks to his makeshift team, the camp manager, and several rangers and trackers gathered around.

"The IV bags will hold him for a while, but he really needs blood. I'm reluctant to play ICU physician here not knowing any of his medical history, but I think I'll need to give him some of these medications and take the chance. Any word on the air rescue team?"

"They haven't answered after my first request," the camp manager responds. "But I hope they're on the way. I'll try again right now."

"He's just a poacher," one of the rangers says bitterly. "He's probably killed numerous rhino. They're becoming extinct because of him. He's not worth all this trouble and expense. Why don't you just let him die like the other two?"

Dr. Merriweather ignores the statement, and Heather says, "I understand your anger, but no matter what he's done, we do not have the right to play God. We do, however, have the responsibility to help where we can. Isn't that what you do in your attempts to save the rhinos?"

Dr. Merriweather looks up at Heather and mutters, "Couldn't have said it better myself."

He then changes the IV bag to the second one and delivers the 0.8 milligrams of atropine in the hopes of increasing his pulse. After five minutes, the pulse has increased to sixty-four, and the blood pressure is now eighty over sixty. As the second IV bag flows in, Dr. Merriweather calculates the dose of epinephrine in his head.

"I want to give him three milligrams in a slow infusion. In a one-to-ten thousand solution, there is one milligram in ten milliliters. I'll need to slowly give him thirty milliliters over five minutes."

With the combination of 1.5 liters of fluids, atropine and epinephrine, the pulse has risen to seventy per minute and the blood pressure a respectable ninety over seventy. The poacher opens his eyes but is minimally responsive and unaware of his surroundings. Dr. Merriweather sees that Robert Malmo and Heather have teamed up to clean and place bandages and dressings on the several wounds the lions inflicted. This reminds him to use the Ancef antibiotic in the kit to treat the contamination in those wounds. He prepares and administers two grams and places it into the IV line.

The overall improvements of the patient are met with sighs of relief and hope, but Dr. Merriweather knows the effects of the atropine and epinephrine will wear off in an hour or so. The man's survival still depends on him receiving blood as quickly as possible.

Just then, the camp manager returns with the news that a fully-equipped rescue team from Johannesburg has arrived in Nelspruit and is already en route via helicopter. Ten minutes later, the now-stable poacher is aboard the rescue chopper and receiving the O-negative blood Dr. Merriweather ordered.

As the chopper lifts off and disappears into the western sky, a celebratory mood breaks out among the group with everyone looking at Dr. Merriweather with a sense of awe.

After humbly waving away their applause, he says, "This was a fine example of a team effort. But, while we can all justifiably feel proud of ourselves for saving that man's life, the overall scene should give us pause for concern. We blame the poachers for killing these animals, but they are doing so—at great risk to their lives—just to provide for their families. This cruel and highly profitable business does not begin with the poacher but with well-hidden criminal masterminds who engineer and perpetuate the myth that the white rhino's horns have medical and social benefits, which is not the case! Unlike animals, who kill for survival, people are slaying the rhinos for one reason: greed. It seems to me that we human beings have evolved a more dangerous trait.

His sobering speech concluded, Robert looks out over the crowd and sees that even the ranger who bitterly spoke earlier is nodding his head in agreement. But it is Robert Malmo who seems the most affected by the ordeal. His eyes meet Dr. Merriweather's for a split second then immediately drop to the floor.

Later that afternoon, the five friends, exhausted by the day's events, prepare to go their separate ways—Dr. Merriweather and Heather to Nelspruit and onto Johannesburg where they will catch a flight back to the United States, and the Malmos to Durban on the Indian Ocean coast then back to their home in Joburg. As everyone exchanges hugs and promises to keep in touch, Merriweather cannot help but wonder at the curious, almost guilty look in Robert Malmo's eyes.

CHAPTER 9
The Uganda Caper Begins

Shortly after midnight, a two-seater plane touches down on a grassy runway in an isolated clearing in the jungle. When it comes to a stop, Big Jim McCullar climbs out of the tiny aircraft and peers down the runway, lit only by two long rows of flaming torches, for the man he is to meet.

"Better be here," Jim mutters, looking at his watch. He has been traveling for several hours, first flying commercially from Johannesburg to Nairobi, followed by this chartered flight to central Uganda.

A moment later, he sees the bright lights of a Range Rover flash, then three men step out of the vehicle, two of them carrying rifles. Jim knows from photographs that the middle one is Nobutu Ingale, the notoriously brutal leader of the resistance to the Ugandan government. Of average height, Nobutu comes only to Jim's shoulder, with very dark skin and curly hair. His short-sleeved, light green combat uniform bears no rank insignia, but he doesn't need one; everyone knows he is their leader. Makeshift they may be, but the members of the Revolutionary Liberation Army are passionately loyal to Nobutu and their cause and have made modest gains over their eight-year existence.

Nobutu barks an order to his men, who rush toward the plane to retrieve Jim's gear. Then, without a welcoming remark or a handshake, the rebel leader approaches Jim.

"I trust you have everything you need for your work here, Mr. McCullar," he says coldly.

Big Jim McCullar glances over his shoulder at the men unloading his weaponry. For this trip, he has brought three .458 rifles and plenty of ammunition; he expects a high utilization rate.

"Yes, I do, and I'll be ready to go by morning.

"Good, we'll plan another try at the herd when they come to the river to drink tomorrow." Nobutu peers at the Australian, sizing him up. "You have quite a reputation, Mr. McCullar. I hope you live up to it."

"Just put me in front of those big tuskers, and I'll bring them down faster than you can sell their tusks."

Jim McCullar knows full well why he is being paid to hunt elephants. Nobutu, whose army is starved for cash and unable to get the weapons they need to carry on their insurrection against the Ugandan government, is trying to raise money through the illegal ivory trade. His largest market is Asia, where the people cherish ivory, from figurines and ornamental inlays to the most popular and coveted status symbol of all—ivory chopsticks that yield up to one thousand US dollars a pair.

Indeed, Nobutu has taken a sizable risk hiring Jim McCullar at his usual two-hundred-thousand-dollar rate, but the loss of the last few native elephant hunters two weeks ago has left him little choice. As they ride to Nobutu's camp, the leader explains that the wounded herd matriarch panicked and led a stampede that killed three men and scattered the herd for more than a week. As he listens to the story, Big Jim doesn't need to be told that Choban, the overly anxious hunter who fired the errant shot that set off the stampede, perished at the hands of Nobutu.

A few minutes later, the Land Rover arrives at the camp. Nobutu issues an order to the driver then turns back to McCullar.

"I'll show you to your quarters, Mr. McCullar. Your gear will be brought to you shortly."

A moment later, they pull up to a rather spacious, round thatched hut. As Jim enters, he sees two cots, one of which is occupied by a seventyish, gray-haired man dressed in safari attire. Behind the man is a makeshift lab with some medical trays, a kerosene-heated culture incubator, and stacks of containers. There is also a small desk over which a kerosene lantern hangs.

The man gets up and extends a hand toward Jim. "You must be my new roommate. Welcome. I'm Randle Lurie."

"Nice to meet you, mate. Jim McCullar here. Professional hunter."

"Oh dear," responds Lurie. "I suspect you're here to resume the elephant slaughter, aren't you?"

"Yes, indeed, mate. Gotta make a living, you know." Big Jim gestures to the paraphernalia behind Lurie. "What are you, some kind of chemist?"

"No, no. I'm a microbiologist and doctor of infectious diseases. I was out on a field mission as part of my sabbatical cataloging subspecies of fungi when…" Lurie lowers his voice. "Nobutu's army seized me and brought me here. I tried to explain to them that I was not part of the government they're trying to overthrow and that I was just out here doing medical research and treating the local villagers. They didn't care about that."

Lurie refrains from telling Big Jim that he is a professor and Chairman of Microbiology at Witwatersrand University or that he is known as a strong advocate for animal rights and the preservation of Africa's wildlife. After three weeks of missing his scheduled radio contact with Albert, Lurie knows his colleagues at the VITS are aware he is missing, and he doesn't want the hunter or the rebels who hired him to interfere with their rescue efforts.

"Tough luck, mate," Jim says. "Then again, they could've killed you."

"They would have, but many in Nobutu's army were suffering from malaria, which is common in these jungles and why I came here in the first place. As long as I treat the ones with malaria and prevent the others from contracting it, they will keep me alive and let me do some of the work I came here to do. Speaking of malaria, you'll need to take the prevention pills each day so you don't come down with it."

Jim gives him a suspicious look. "These pills wouldn't have any side effects, would they, Doctor? Big Jim's got a lot to do here, and I got to be in tiptop shape to do it."

"No, no, my dear boy. It's called doxycycline." Lurie walks to his stash of pills and pulls out a bottle to show Big Jim. "It's harmless to humans but kills even the most resistant plasmodium. Plasmodium falciparum, that's the parasite group that causes malaria, you know. Be sure to take one each day. Almost everyone here does, including me."

"Not me, Doc."

"Mr. McCullar, I implore you. Think of it as an immune booster. It will help you fight off all types of infections."

"Immune booster! Do you think this fine specimen needs an immune booster? My immune system is as good as it comes. You can ask the B and B girls about that. No, Doc," Jim says, shaking his head, "my body is my temple, and I'm not going to pollute it with chemicals. Now you just let old Jim prepare for tomorrow's hunt while you get back to your jungle bugs."

Professor Lurie, angered and forlorn at the thought of his new roommate murdering his most beloved animals, puts away the jar of doxycycline along with another medicine he didn't have time to offer.

CHAPTER 10
The Hunt

By sunup the following morning, Jim and Nobutu are in a Land Rover, rumbling toward a clearing frequented by various elephant herds. Although Nobutu's men have cleared a road-like pathway through the brush, the ride is a bumpy one, taking them through large puddles and over numerous rocks.

Fifteen minutes later, they find themselves at the clearing, which is now devoid of elephants. As Nobutu converses with the driver, Jim gets out and quietly begins surveying the landscape. His attention is drawn to the west end, where a jut of trees encroaches into the clearing and is in the direct pathway to the river.

He walks to the area and stoops down to examine several clumps of elephant dung, many the size of a grapefruit. He seeks out the largest and moistest clumps and breaks some open to see if any dung beetle or dung beetle larvae are present. Seeing none, he announces that the elephants were last there between three and five o'clock the previous afternoon and that there are maybe eight or twelve over four tons and would therefore presumably have tusks of sufficient size for Nobutu. Jim now turns his attention to the sky and tests the winds.

"This is perfect. The wind is now coming out of the north but will be switching around to the east by afternoon. I'll set up in the trees to the west. The angle of the sun will place a glare in their eyes, and the stand will be downwind of the elephants. They won't know I'm here."

"So you think you can get a kill today?" Nobutu asks.

"Hell, I'll get you two or three if they're not still spooked by the fiasco your man created a couple weeks ago."

Nobutu ignores the snide comment as they climb back into the Land Rover for the ride back to camp. Unsure if Jim's braggadocio is based on truth or is just an empty boast, he keeps a close eye on the big Aussie, looking for any hint of uncertainty in his body language. He sees none.

Back at camp, Jim returns to his hut to find Dr. Lurie gone. He spends several minutes loading his rifles and arranging his ammunition when the scent of roasting meat reaches his nostrils. Realizing how hungry he is, he follows the smell to the center of camp, where the cook's tent is located. Some seventy troops are mingling around the stoves and small fires. Some are just sitting around talking and gesturing in various dialects, only a few of which he doesn't understand.

He enters the cook's tent and sees the only two women in the camp roasting meat over an open fire. He helps himself to some of it and carries his plate outside. The meat is hopefully kudu or impala but possibly monkey or chimpanzee. In any event, he finds it quite tasty.

After eating his fill, Jim meanders into several storage huts. Most are filled with rifles, ammunition, hand grenades and rocket launchers, the common armaments of African rebels. In the next tent, he finds Professor Lurie with an atomizer spraying a small stash of remaining elephant tusks that Nobutu hopes will be added to by Jim's kill later today.

Big Jim taps the brim of his Aussie hat upward. "What're you up to, Doc?"

"Oh, just disinfecting these tusks before they're shipped out. You know elephants often carry the anthrax bacillus and sometimes even Yersinia pestis.

"What's that?"

Lurie pauses in his task. "Well, you've heard of anthrax. It can be a bad, potentially lethal skin or lung infection. And Yersinia pestis is the bacteria that caused the plaque." Seeing Jim's blank stare, Lurie adds, "You've heard of the bubonic plague of the fourteenth century…? It was called the Black Death…?"

"No, and I don't want to hear about it. But these babies look pretty clean to me." Jim reaches out to stroke one of the tusks.

"Oh, no, no, don't touch them. You'll contaminate them all over again, and my disinfectant may irritate your skin. Now, be sure to wash your hands thoroughly." To head off another diatribe about Big Jim's invincibility, he warns, "You wouldn't want a rash to interfere with your shooting, now, would you?"

Jim leaves the tent and Professor Lurie to his disinfection duties to take a short nap before setting up for the elephant kill. However, he does take the professor's suggestion to wash his hands at a nearby water bucket. There is no way his hunt is going to be waylaid by some rash.

***

By three o'clock, Jim is perched ten feet off the ground in a large Jackalberry tree at the west end of the clearing he scouted earlier. He has one rifle in hand and two others perched beside him on a nearby branch. These are his modified side-by-side barrel, .458 caliber, which allow him to get two shots off without reloading.

He told Nobutu and the rest of his so-called elephant hunters to stay a mile or so back so as not to spook the herd. As he predicted, the wind has shifted to the east so that he is now downwind of the oncoming herd. To disguise his scent further, he has sprayed his clothes and exposed skin with a commercial "scent be gone" spray used commonly by deer hunters in the US.

He looks out over the clearing and gauges his "kill zone," which he estimates to be about thirty yards in front of him. He will let the matriarch pass through the kill zone so that those that follow her will not be likely to reverse their course and flee back eastward.

"You can't kill an elephant by shooting him in the butt," he mutters cheerfully.

Experienced at killing elephants by legal herd culling activities years earlier, Jim knows he must get a forward entry brain shot. A side shot on an elephant's skull will only wound it and allow the animal to escape and require hours of tracking to find, not to mention the danger of approaching an enraged, wounded elephant to finish it off. Jim knows he must first be patient, then fast and accurate.

His strategy laid out to his satisfaction, he settles in for the part of the hunt he finds most difficult: waiting. It is said that everyone has his demons, and Big Jim McCullar is no exception. They creep into his mind whenever he is idle, which is why is he so seldom allows himself to be so.

James Francis McCullar was born in Alice Springs, a remote town in Northern Australia. He never knew his mother, who died in childbirth, a fact of which he was not aware until he was twelve years old. The thought that he had caused the death of a mother he never knew is one that James was never able to understand; nor was he allowed to forget it. To Jim's father, an abusive drunkard who managed the family ranch, James was a constant reminder of his poor lot in life. He forced Jim and his older brother Alistair to do the lion's share of the work and often beat them mercilessly for the smallest infractions or failures to complete their chores.

James' growing resentment of his father boiled over when Alistair committed suicide in response to a particularly vicious beating. He vividly recalls the day when, while feeding their cattle close to the barn, he heard a single loud pop. Recognizing it immediately as a gunshot, he raced into the barn to find Alistair with a small entrance wound in his right temple and a larger exit wound in his left. The sight of his dead brother, the one he looked up to and who was the substitute for a real father, would haunt him for the rest of his life.

James stuck around just long enough to see Alistair buried then ran away from the ranch. He supported himself with a variety of odd jobs, including those that involved hunting, which allowed him to hone his skills with rifles, knives, and pistols. He lived from hand to mouth for several years before hiring on with a crew of mercenaries who, among other things, protected men of wealth. With his size and superior abilities, he quickly became their leader, and Big Jim McCullar was born. Since then, he has enjoyed a very lucrative career working for some of the world's most nefarious criminals. But, in the end, the only interest he has served is his own.

An hour passes before the first elephant enters the clearing on its far east end, followed closely by two others, including the matriarch. Tentative at first, they stop to graze on some fresh shoots of grass and nearby tree branches. Then, as adult elephants require ten to fifteen gallons of water each day, caution gives way to thirst. Jim watches as the matriarch lumbers ever so slowly but directly toward the river, and toward him, followed by the rest of the herd. Jim realizes his earlier concerns were unfounded; the matriarch, the very same wounded by Choban's ill-fated shot, shows no caution as she enters the kill zone.

As she comes closer, Jim focuses his attention on several

big tuskers behind her that are just about to enter the kill zone. Ever so slowly and quietly, Jim raises his first gun. He plans to get two shots off with his first gun before grabbing the second one, which is already loaded and ready to go.

Just then, four big, tusked female elephants, three of which have little ones beside them, enter the kill zone. He aims at the closest one and slowly and steadily squeezes the trigger. There is a sharp crack, and the elephant slumps to her knees. Before the echo of the first shot can be heard, a second crack rings out. Another elephant down, then a third and a fourth in rapid succession. Four elephants in eight seconds, each with a single shot. Nobutu and his men, far off now, hear the trumpeting and literally feel the ground tremble as the panicked herd stampedes back eastward with the matriarch frantically trying to overtake the rest in order to resume her leadership duties.

The rebels speed toward the scene, hopeful that one of the shots brought down an elephant or, if luck was with them and Jim McCullar is as good as his reputation, two elephants. Arriving at the clearing and only having heard four shots, they are in awe at the scene before them: four elephants down and Big Jim McCullar standing beside the biggest with a look of victory on his smug face.

Stepping toward the Australian, Nobutu offers a rare flash of yellowish teeth. But his men are truly shocked when he joyfully embraces the strange white man and remarks, "I didn't believe you were for real. I do now, Mr. McCullar."

Nobutu's men immediately begin cutting around the base of each tusk, which is actually a modified tooth that in humans would be termed an upper lateral incisor. Since a tusk has a relatively short root for its length, it doesn't take long to remove the eight tusks. Transporting them, however, proves to be a much more arduous task. First, it takes three men to carry each fifty-kilogram tusk to the Land Rover. Then, since the vehicle can only transport two tusks at a time, they must make four separate trips back and forth to camp.

As the tusks are being carried to the Land Rover, choice meat sections are also cut from each elephant for the next few day's dinners and for smoking. They leave behind a macabre scene of hacked, tuskless elephant carcasses that would turn most westerner's stomachs. To Nobutu and his men, however, it signifies survival; to Jim McCullar, it is merely a day's work.

CHAPTER 11
Old George

After just one week, Big Jim has decimated the local elephant population. Every elephant with a reasonably-sized tusk has been slaughtered, and those that are left have scattered. Drunk on power and the thought of a huge financial windfall, Big Jim fully devotes himself to producing as much ivory as possible. He queries Nobutu's men about any nearby small rivers with grasslands on each side, and the two who speak English tell him of such a place just twenty-five kilometers away.

"Okay, mates, get your vehicles ready. We're going after some freebies and some easy pickings."

Within an hour, four Land Rovers, one carrying Big Jim and Nobutu, are heading west. There's an extra man in each of the other three vehicles. They will help collect the tusks Big Jim has promised. All the rebels, including Nobutu, are intrigued by the Australian's boast of *easy pickings and freebies.* They have no idea about what he's planning, but they've already learned not to doubt Big Jim, who has exceeded their expectations in delivering a bounty of ivory. Nobutu's men also welcome a break from the drudgery of the camp and their leader's endless military training exercises.

Ninety minutes later, the caravan reaches the small river. There are no elephants in sight, and once again, Big Jim gets out and begins surveying the terrain. He points to the south, and the men get back into the Land Rovers. After another half-hour, they come to the place where the river widens and the flow of water slows down. There are also numerous turn-backs, flows, and pools where a marsh and rich grassland have developed. With the vehicles moving slowly amidst the knee-length, rich, green grass, Nobutu's men see several small herds of zebra, impala, and wildebeest grazing on the tender shoots, but no elephants.

All eyes turn toward Big Jim.

"You don't see elephants, do you, mates?"

The rebels shake their heads in confusion, all save Nobutu, who merely narrows his eyes at the Australian. Has Big Jim finally failed in one of his boasts, or is he setting them up? Were his previous successes an attempt to gain Nobutu's confidence so that he could arrange an ambush with the corrupt government the rebels are trying to depose? A rare flash of fear erupts in Nobutu's mind. He clutches the pistol strapped to his belt.

"Get out of your vehicles," Big Jim says, breaking the tense silence, "and walk toward the tallest grass up ahead."

Two men dutifully jump out of each vehicle and begin combing the tall grass. Less than five minutes later, Nobutu and the others hear their shouts of excitement.

Two men rush back to the Land Rover, where Big Jim and Nobutu, still clutching his gun, are standing together next to the front grill plate. Big Jim flashes them a knowing smile.

"Mr. McCullar," one of them says breathlessly, "there are bones—elephant bones, many, many, white from the sun! There are many elephant tusks, too. I counted twelve, maybe more. Most in good condition."

Nobutu looks at Jim McCullar in wonderment. "An elephant burial ground? I thought that was just legend. How'd you know, Mr. McCullar?"

"Oh, Big Jim knows many things. But are we going to talk, or are we going to gather up the freebies I promised? Not all the tusks will be useable, only the ones that came from elephants that died in the past year or two. Look them over, Nobutu. You should take the best ones back to camp today and flag the rest of the good ones for your men to retrieve later."

Nobutu nods curtly at the Australian, then orders the rest back into the tall grass. As they go about their task, his men rave of the success of their treasure hunt and their growing admiration for the great white hunter. Nobutu remains silent, however, as he tries to figure out how Big Jim knew elephant burial grounds weren't just legend and where to find one. One that has now produced twenty-one *freebie* tusks for him.

Big Jim sits on the hood of the vehicle smoking a celebratory Cuban Robusto cigar he brought with him from Joburg. He knows that, like many legends, the elephant burial ground is partly rooted. In fact, years ago, an African animal behaviorist gave him quite the education on elephants.

Most, he said, die a natural death from starvation and malnutrition. He also said that throughout their lives, elephants have only six teeth on each side of their jaws. In a line like a conveyor belt, the ones from the back slowly push out and replace worn ones in the front. Around age forty-five, the last set of teeth are in place. As this final set of teeth wear down from the elephant's typical diet of tree branches and coarse grasses mixed with sand, they can't chew efficiently and therefore don't eat enough of these plants to sustain them. They lose weight and strength. They can no longer keep up with the herd, and they separate, instinctively migrating to an area of abundant water and the more tender and chewable grasses, to live out their final days. Eventually, unable to chew even these tender grasses, they weaken further and die, their bodies eaten and scattered by scavengers such as hyenas and vultures. In the end, only their bones and tusks of ivory remain, mingled with others of their kind. Hence, the elephant burial ground.

No one could accuse Big Jim McCullar of not being a good listener.

***

Rambling back toward camp, the Land Rovers come upon a young bull elephant of twenty-eight years courting and chasing a female in heat. The young male is in musth, a period of increased reproductive hormones and accompanying aggressive behavior. The bull's testosterone-enhanced desire is displayed by the streaming of a sweat-like fluid running down his cheeks, from the opening of a stress gland in front of each one of his big ears. His intent to mate is also broadcast by a substance dribbling from his penis and a secretion of pheromones from his loins. He unsuccessfully tries to mount the female, who rebukes his overtures by moving away. The frustrated, mature but inexperienced male flaps his large ears and, with a loud trumpet, trots after her.

The man audience in the Land Rovers chuckles at the scene, one they've witnessed many times before. Their light-hearted interlude is broken by an even louder trumpeting followed by an even bigger bull elephant of about forty-five years of age emerging from a nearby stand of trees. He, too, is in a state of musth and displays the same outward signs.

Big Jim knows what's about to happen and instructs the drivers to move their Land Rovers back, away from the two behemoths.

"Boys, this ought to be a good one—a real rumble in the jungle," he says, a nod to the famous boxing match between Muhammed Ali and George Foreman in Zaire in 1974. "I'm betting on that big boy, Old George."

As Big Jim predicted, the testosterone-enraged, younger bull isn't about to give up his prize. He charges toward Old George with ears now pinned back and trumpeting loudly. Old George responds in kind, and the two meet, butting heads in a monstrous pushing match. Loud trumpeting continues as a cloud of Ugandan dust billows upward to shroud the two combatants. Like two sumo wrestlers, each tries to push the other back or upend his foe. The monumental back-and-forth struggle continues for about ten minutes. Then the larger size and greater experience of Old George begins to show. Time and time again, he pushes his foe back. But though the younger bull tires, he won't retreat. He persists now against the odds in the age-old battle to pass on his genes to the next generation. It proves to be a fatal mistake.

In one backward push, the younger bull's side is turned, and the long, pointed tusks of Old George pierces his side, breaking ribs and puncturing a lung. The young bull collapses, mortally wounded. As he lies on his side with a bloody mist shooting out of a gaping hole in the other side, his victorious adversary trots off, trumpeting in search of the female.

No sympathy is felt by the human onlookers, nor is there any introspection about the cruelty of Mother Nature. Instead, they rush to the dying elephant to finish him off and gain two more freebie tusks. This time, perhaps to diminish some of the hero worship lavished on Big Jim, Nobutu takes out his nine-millimeter and delivers a close-range brain shot that sends an agonal tremor through the young bull. With a dying move, the young bull reflexively raises his head and blurts out one last blood-splattering trumpet from his trunk. In doing so, he knocks Nobutu, his driver, and Big Jim off their feet.

Each rolls over to get up and chuckles at the near miss. However, their humor is quickly interrupted by a louder and more sustained trumpeting followed by the sight of Old George returning. Whether he was spurned by the same female or came back to challenge the source of the renewed trumpeting, Old George means business once again.

Big Jim is quick to realize this is no mock charge. Old George's ears are pinned back, not flapping as they would be in a mock charge, and his trumpeting is louder and longer. He's also quick to realize that his .458 caliber rifle was thrown more than ten feet away by the death throes of the young bull. He makes a dive for his other rifle, dubbed the Queen Mother, and stabilizes it on the dead elephant's chest. While postured in this awkward sitting position, he gains a quick sight, a bead on the only area that will bring down the beast. He pulls a steady and smooth squeeze on the trigger. Due to his awkward stance, Big Jim is lurched back by the recoil just enough to save him. Old George collapses from the single hurried shot and skids over the body of his vanquished foe, the point of his tusks stopping within inches of Big Jim's face.

As the other men look on in shocked silence, Big Jim pulls himself into a standing position and calmly says, "Now that was a close one, eh mates?"

Some of the men sigh in relief. Others break out in nervous laughter. Some even start to wonder if Big Jim is no ordinary man but the stuff of legends. All, however, are more than ready to harvest the four remaining tusks and hightail it back to camp before any other mishaps befall them.

Chapter 12
The Outbreak

It has now been five days since the big harvest of tusks from the elephant burial grounds. Nobutu's camp should be full of jubilation about the recent influx of ivory and meat, but it's not. Of the nearly eighty fighters under Nobutu's command, forty-two have contracted malaria. It seems these forty-two have forgone Professor Lurie's doxycycline pills and instead sought out the camp's cooks, both of whom double as traditional healers.

In present-day Africa, such healers aren't the witch doctors of Hollywood lore but are actually licensed and certified in traditional healing. They're required to practice their brand of healing only after their patient has been seen by a real medical doctor. One of the cooks, however, has shirked this duty and counseled the soldiers who were suspicious of Western medicine to throw away Lurie's daily preventative and treatments pills.

With about half the camp ill and morale being at an all-time low, Nobutu desperately seeks out Professor Lurie's help.

"Mr. Ingale," he replies, "your troops are in the early stages of the disease, which is why their symptoms are limited to fever and weakness. However, left untreated, the disease will progress to coma and death. I have told your men this, yet they continue to refuse my pills. I have even forced them into their mouths, but they just spit them out. I'm really at a loss."

"No doubt they view pills as unique to Western medicine and therefore suspect," Nobutu says. "Dr. Lurie, are you able to inject the medicine?"

Professor Lurie's eyes widen. "Yes! I can break open the capsules and dissolve the doxycycline in water and some alcohol. I have only a few needles and syringes, but I guess I can sterilize them over an open flame. The injections will hurt, but by golly, they should work."

"Okay," the rebel leader replies, "then I have an idea."

Lurie finds himself excited over the prospect of practicing real field medicine and curing many individuals, even those who have killed his beloved elephants. On Nobutu's orders, he calculates the required number of injections then dutifully begins the task of making two hundred ninety-four doses, each two hundred milligrams of doxycycline that he will administer every day for one full week.

While Professor Lurie prepares the injections, Nobutu seeks out the second cook, whom he has known for a long time and has even sought out for the treatment of minor ailments in the past.

"Magda, you must help my troops," he implores. "They have malaria, and they're refusing to take the medicine our doctor gives them. I can't afford to lose my army. If this happens, our cause will be lost, and you'll never get the revenge you seek against the government."

Magda, a short African native, knows malaria and the sickness it causes very well. She also harbors a deep hatred for the Ugandan Army that pillaged her village, raped and killed her sisters, murdered anyone who didn't flee, and burnt their homes to the ground. Furthermore, she appreciates the powers of Western medicine, as she once hoped to become a nurse or even a doctor. This dream, however, was thwarted by the government, which resisted educating women and barred them from those professions. Seeking the next best thing, she studied and passed the certification test for traditional medicine. So she knows exactly what to do to help Nobutu's cause.

"Nobutu, bring all the sick ones to me. I'll perform a ritual. They'll take the medicine of the doctor after that, I promise."

At six that evening, in the fading light of a steamy, hot day, the stricken members of the camp gather in a large semicircle. Some are able to sit cross-legged, while others are propped up against benches made of logs, resting on large stones. Despite their weakness and fever, they're set to pay keen attention in the hopes of receiving the direction on how to rid themselves of illness. Several feet away, Nobutu, Dr. Lurie, and Big Jim stand to observe the scene, each wondering if the ritual will be successful, each with his own reasons for hoping it is.

Kneeling on a bright red cloth at the head of the semicircle, Magda bears little resemblance to the woman who prepares their meals each day. Her outfit for the ritual is also bright red and has black and white images of various animals on it. She wears a headband of brown impala fur that has a midline tuft of the animal's white tail and is clutching a two-foot wooden rod with red and white beads at the handle and the long black hairs of a male zebra at its end. At her feet is a collection of small animal bones, a few seashells, a domino, and even a pair of dice. The bones are from a female and male of each of the common species in the territory, twenty-six in all. The non-animal items are to guide her in interpreting the meanings and predictions of the animal bones as they will come to lay.

Without preamble, Magda begins the ritual. After a full ten minutes of repetitive incantations, she shakes her wooden rod and seems to put herself into a trance. There are beads of perspiration collecting on her forehead and running down her smooth black cheeks. She then abruptly stops and gathers up all the animal bones and non-animal items in front of her. The group is silent, though a palpable feeling of expectation pervades the air. Magda can barely hold all the items in her hands, yet, with one final incantation, she manages to throw them down on the cloth. For what seems to be hours, Magda stares wide-eyed at the bones, trying to glean their meaning. Finally, speaking in the local Nyan Korean language of Uganda, she begins to explain her reading of the spread.

Nobutu interprets for Professor Lurie and Big Jim. "She is telling them that to rid themselves of their fever and regain their strength, they must first find a green cloth and soak it with water. They must then take it to an old white man in a white gown. He'll make them suffer with the quills of a porcupine. But if they're brave enough to endure it, the medicine from the hairs of the porcupine's ancestors will make then well again."

Professor Lurie draws back in surprise as he realizes Magda's interpretation centers around him. He recalls that he indeed has a white lab coat in his equipment bag, and the porcupine quills refer to his injection needles. Was the woman's mention of these things a coincidence, or evidence of a true gift?

As night falls, Magda kneels, motionless, with her head now down on the red cloth. With a renewed sense of hope, the stricken leave or are carried off, each seeking a green cloth.

"What's so humorous, mate?" Big Jim asks when he sees the smile cross Nobutu's face.

"They won't have to go far for the cloths," he replies. "Though they don't always wear them, green headbands are standard issue for all my soldiers."

***

The next day, all forty-two of the stricken arrive at Professor Lurie's tent. When his turn comes, each man bows in respect to the good doctor and hands him a wet, green cloth then allows Nobutu and Big Jim to take hold of him. Dressed in his white lab coat, Professor Lurie cleans off an injection site on the upper arm and jabs the syringe into the thick muscle. The injection is indeed painful due to the crude makeup of the antibiotic solution and its alcohol solvent. However, each man, buoyed by Magda's prophecy of the man with the powerful porcupine quills, bravely endures the pain in the hopes of getting well.

This scene is repeated daily for a full seven days, at the end of which all the sickened individuals have made a near-full recovery, and Nobutu and both his medical providers breathe a collective sigh of relief. For Professor Lurie, the return to direct patient treatment has brought him a sense of satisfaction he hasn't felt in years. For Magda, it has been a rare chance to work alongside a doctor of Western medicine and to utilize her own culture to help others. The crises now over, she returns to her cook tent filled with a combination of pride and sadness over what might have been had she been allowed to attend medical school.

CHAPTER 13
The Road to Mombasa

Nobutu Ingale wakes up to the crack of rifle fire followed by the shrill and mocking calls from a troop of baboons within the camp. More rifle fire, and the squawking sounds stop. It seems Big Jim McCullar is engaging in target practice again.

Grunting in annoyance, Nobutu swings his legs over the side of his cot. The Aussie's continued presence at the camp has begun to grate on his nerves. Ever since their successful campaign left the area nearly devoid of elephants, Big Jim McCullar has slipped into boredom. As he waits to collect his fee, he occupies himself primarily with eating the soldiers' rations and killing whatever creature he can find. Nobutu is grateful for the 108 new tusks, most of which have already been shipped off to Mombasa, a coastal city in Kenya, for storage before their trip over the Indian Ocean. The rebel leader grows tired of his troops' respect and admiration for the great white hunter, not to mention the arrogance of Big Jim himself.

Nobutu also finds himself wishing he could dispense with the old man Lurie and would have done so already if he wasn't afraid of another malaria outbreak.

Perhaps, Nobutu thinks, this is the reason for his restlessness of late. Accustomed to having complete control over the camp, he now feels beholden to not one but two foreigners. Suddenly, the solution is clear—it's time to break camp.

He reaches out to his most trusted lieutenant to inform him of the plan. Nobutu, joined by Big Jim and Dr. Lurie, will go to Mombasa to collect cash for the tusks while the lieutenant relocates the rest of the troops to Gulu in Northern Uganda. Once his business in Mombasa is concluded, Nobutu will join them, presumably with newly recruited troops and desperately needed weapons and ammunition.

The lieutenant nods and rushes off to set the plans in motion. A few hours later, two Land Rovers, one carrying Nobutu, Big Jim, and Dr. Lurie, and the other carrying three of his other best lieutenants, head eastward, beginning the twenty-one-hour drive from the Ugandan jungle to the Kenyan coastal city of Mombasa.

***

It's no accident that Nobutu chose Mombasa to store his ivory. Being a relatively small port, it's not a place where one would see oil supertankers or cruise ships packed with tourists, but it is perfectly capable of handling hundred-ton vessels ideal for shipping things under the radar. Customs control at the docks is apathetic or can be bought off at a pittance, making it ideal for transporting

Nobutu's ivory to the waiting arms of distributors in China.

First, though, they must make it to Mombasa in one piece. His men, who drive in shifts so they can drive through the night, take a route that will minimize their chances of detection by government troops. The chatter of Nobutu's men can be heard over the roaring of the engine, but the back seat, where the rebel leader sits with Big Jim and Professor Lurie, is conspicuously silent. Each man is lost in his own thoughts, with the rebel leader planning the rise of his army, the Australian wondering whether Nobutu will try to screw him out of his money, and Professor Lurie hoping the caravan will be stopped by someone who will return him to his university before his usefulness to the rebels expires.

Early the next afternoon, they arrive, stiff and exhausted, at the coastal city and head to the warehouse where the ivory has been stored for the past few weeks. Nobutu would have preferred to go alone to meet his man, who had gone ahead with the shipment weeks earlier and has been guarding it ever since, but Big Jim and Professor Lurie insist on accompanying him. Both men, Nobutu admits, have valid reasons. Big Jim wants to tally his cut of the proceeds, and Professor Lurie wants to disinfect the glistening white ivory tusks one more time before shipment.

Satisfied that all the tusks are there, Nobutu pulls his man aside to the back of the warehouse and gives him instructions in Swahili while Professor Lurie goes about spraying the tusks one final time. As always, Big Jim takes the opportunity to survey his surroundings, including all the exits, as well as any signs that Nobutu is planning to turn on him.

His business in the warehouse concluded, the rebel leader returns, along with his other men, and leads Jim and Lurie through the dingy town adjacent to the dock. As they walk through the rows of broken-down shanties constructed of broken plywood walls and corrugated tin roofs with more than a few holes, even Big Jim McCullar is taken aback by the sights and smells. Barefoot children, clad only in white underpants and sporting the protruding bellies indicative of malnutrition, play in streets strewn with rotting garbage. Many of them have scars on their feet and faces from past infections while others have open sores at which flies gather. Uncaged chickens scurry about, stopping every now and again to scavenge the heaps of trash.

Overcome by the stench, Dr. Lurie feels his stomach churn and places a handkerchief over his nose. Each step becomes a battle to keep from vomiting, passing out, or both, and it is with great relief when Nobutu announces that they have arrived at the shanty he and Jim will share.

"Make yourselves comfortable," Nobutu says, gesturing toward the door.

Big Jim eyes him. "And where are you staying, mate?"

Nobutu smiles coldly. "Close by."

Lurie and Big Jim walk into the shanty, which has a dirt floor, two cots, and four chairs. Next to them is a pile of some of Lurie's equipment, no doubt placed there earlier by some of Nobutu's men. The shanty is about one-third the size of their thatched hut back at the camp in Uganda, but compared with the scene outside, it feels like a refuge. There is no electricity, and the only light comes from the moonbeam streaming in through a small window. Lurie watches curiously as the Australian claims one of the two cots and moves it into the center of the tiny room. As he sets his back down on the other cot, Professor Lurie is overwhelmed again, this time by a feeling of dread. He's unsure whether he'll be killed or freed, but whatever the case, he's sure it'll happen tomorrow. He also finds himself unable to keep silent any longer.

"Mr. McCullar, you're not planning to continue killing elephants, are you? After Nobutu pays you, I mean. Because I can assure you this country can't afford to lose anymore." Greeted with Big Jim's uninterested stare, he adds, "Did you know that every country from Sudan down to Botswana and Tanzania has lost more than seventy percent of their elephants to ivory poachers like Nobutu. Like you. Is there anything I can say or do to dissuade you?"

"Not necessary, mate. After we're done here, I'm headed over to the States for a well-deserved holiday." He pulls his cot into the center of the tiny room, then sets his bag down and begins rummaging through it for a change of clothes. "I hear American women are very willing to hook up with a man with an Australian accent and other *attributes* if you know what I mean. I'm thinking Miami Beach will be my first stop. Women there are supposed to be gorgeous." He looks at the dejected-looking Dr. Lurie. "I'll be back eventually, though, and when I do, I'll hook up with a bigger ivory operation, not this half-assed thing

Nobutu is running. He's small-time, a petty gangster who thinks he's going to change his country by overturning the current corrupt leaders for new ones who'll be just as corrupt."

"Surely, with your skills, there's another way to earn a living?" Lurie says.

"Well, I could go back to Syria or Libya. Those oil boys pay big bucks for protection there. But those areas are crazy now, and Big Jim isn't into unnecessary risks." He chuckles. "Elephants don't shoot back, mate."

As he digests the Australian's vile words, Professor Lurie finds his inner conservation locked in battle with his inner physician. The physician wins out.

"Well then, I can't say I wish you luck, but at least I can help you prevent infection. I saw you touching and combing over some of the tusks. You don't have to take my immune-boosting pills, but at least let me spray your hands."

Big Jim shakes his head. "Not now, Doc. I suspect that our last night together may not be a quiet one. I suggest you pull your cot into the middle where mine is and cover yourself up." He looks Lurie in the eye. "And, Doc, sleep lightly tonight."

Lurie hurriedly undresses and slides into bed, Big Jim's warning weighing heavily on his mind and reinforcing his own feeling of dread.

At 3:00 a.m., Professor Lurie is still wide awake. Wondering if his roommate is also awake, he turns to his left side and squints in the dim light at Big Jim's cot. There's no movement, so perhaps Big Jim isn't as concerned as he let on. Then Lurie notices that despite the hot, humid night, the cot is fully covered with a blanket. He also notes that the contour under the covers is angulated and square in shape, not like that of a human body but more like some of his own equipment. Finally, he concludes rather sheepishly that he must have dozed off after all. But where is Mr. McCullar?

He looks around to see his roommate sitting still and somewhat camouflaged by Lurie's lab equipment. Professor Lurie is about to speak, when he sees Jim bring his index finger up to his lips. Nearly paralyzed with fear, the professor forces himself to take several deep breaths, then pulls his blanket over his head.

Thirty minutes of eerie silence later, the door opens with a loud crash. Lurie stifles a gasp as he feels a long, fleshy object hit his blanket and career off. Then another hits Jim's cot. Afraid to remove his blanket, he just lies there listening to a rustling sound outside followed by a native voice pleading, "No, no, no, Bawana, have mercy, have mercy." He then hears screaming and the sounds of commotion, this time around Jim's cot. There's more moaning and weeping, followed by two thuds. Once again, the shanty is silent except for the heavy breathing coming from the floor around Jim's cot.

"It's a good thing you put that blanket over you, Professor. It saved your life. You can take it off now."

Professor Lurie removes the blanket to see big Jim standing above him with a blood-coated machete in his hand. Fearing the hunter is going to use it on him, the professor clamps his eyes shut and puts his hands up, a futile attempt to fend off an attack. He then hears the soft sound of Jim chuckling.

"Really, mate?"

Realizing he's in no danger from Big Jim, Lurie opens his eyes and looks around the shanty to see what the commotion was about. There are two snake heads chopped off, with their bodies still squirming nearby. He then focuses his gaze on the source of the heavy breathing. It's Nobutu's first lieutenant, shaking and whimpering in a fetal position.

"Jim, what happened?"

"That bastard Nobutu sent this guy to trap these black mambas and do us in. He opened the door and threw them on our cots, knowing that the snakes would strike as soon as they hit. Of course, he stuck around in case he had to finish us off himself. He didn't count on Big Jim waiting for him, though. I made sure he and the snakes got reacquainted. He got bit. He won't last long."

Jim doesn't need to tell the professor about black mambas, the fast-moving and deadliest snake in all of Africa, if not the entire world. No one has ever survived a full black mamba bite, even with prompt medical care.

Sure enough, within five minutes, the lieutenant goes into massive convulsions. When the convulsions cease, he stops breathing and quietly dies on the floor of the shanty.

"Guess we have ourselves a houseguest, huh, mate?" Big Jim quips.

Professor Lurie says nothing and lies back down on the cot, unsure if he'll ever sleep again.

✻✻✻

Early the next morning, Nobutu arrives at the warehouse expecting to meet his Asian contact and collect his money. Instead, standing near the entrance is Big Jim McCullar and Professor Lurie. At Big Jim's feet lies the body of Nobutu's most valued lieutenant.

"Nobutu, old boy, you seem surprised to see us. Now why's that? Maybe you put too much stock in your choice of weapons." Big Jim throws the two snake heads at his feet. "And in the men you send to do your dirty work." With a menacing snarl, Jim lifts the lieutenant's corpse from the ground and throws it at Nobutu's feet. "I'll wager that you don't know how well a voice echoes around this warehouse, mate. I'll also wager that you think whites don't know Swahili."

Professor Lurie stands there, his eyes darting back and forth between the two adversaries. For a beat, he considers making a run for it but quickly dismisses the thought. Even if he did get away, where would he go? And to whom? Like it or not, he is at the mercy of whoever wins this standoff.

"McCullar," Nobutu says, "I see you didn't bring your

handguns. Rather peculiar. I would've thought you were smarter than to bring a knife to a gunfight."

Nobutu goes to draw his weapon but is stopped by what feels like a punch to his chest. He looks down, shocked to see McCullar's nine-inch knife buried up to its handle.

"What was that, mate?" McCullar mockingly places his hand to his ear.

Before hiring Big Jim McCullar, the rebel leader had heard quite a bit about his many talents. Unfortunately, he forgot that the Aussie can throw a knife with the speed and precision of a Las Vegas performer. In less than ten seconds, the hole in his heart pours enough blood into the chest wall for Nobutu to lose consciousness and collapse. It only takes a few seconds more for him to die.

It takes another hour before the Asian distributor shows up at the warehouse. When he sees the two corpses lying on the floor, his expression registers only mild surprise.

"Who's the seller?" he asks, though his gaze automatically goes to the Aussie.

"You're looking at him, mate."

The Asian nods, and in less than thirty minutes, Big Jim has closed the deal. Nobutu's ivory for a cool nine hundred thousand American dollars.

With that, the three men step out into the warm, bright Mombasa morning. As the distributor instructs his crew to begin loading the tusks onto the ship destined for Hong Kong, Big Jim turns to Lurie and hands him a one-hundred-thousand-dollar stack of cash.

"Your cut for acting as a decoy, Doc. At your age, you better spend it while you can."

Lurie looks with wide eyes from the money to Jim, unsure of what surprises him more, that he's been given the money or that he's been allowed to live.

"And you as well, Big Jim. You as well."

CHAPTER 14
The Chinese Wedding and Much More

The next afternoon and half a world away, Dr. Robert Merriweather, Chief of Oral and Maxillofacial Surgery at the University of Miami's Miller School of Medicine, is seeing the last of his patients for the day. They are Mark and Michael Eng, Chinese-American twins he has been treating for fifteen years. When they were just six years old, Dr. Merriweather diagnosed each with basal cell nevus syndrome, and over the past decade and a half has removed six cysts from Mark's jaws and seven from the jaws of his brother. Today, after conducting their annual examination and reviewing their cone beam CT scans, he has pronounced the Eng is free of new cysts and unlikely to develop any more. This is great news to the twins, who recently received their master's degrees in industrial engineering from the University of Miami and are looking forward to promising futures.

In fact, they announce to Dr. Merriweather that they've both been hired by Ryder Trucking Company to work on a safer and more efficient fuel pumping system and to prepare for a possible conversion to electric-powered trucks.

"You're kidding!" Merriweather grins broadly. "My son Ryan has worked for Ryder for the past eight years. He manages the Redco Division, which is involved with their national fuel distribution. I guess you'll see him on occasion. What a coincidence."

Frank Eng, the boys' father and a professor of Chemical Engineering at the university's main Coral Gables campus, sticks his head around the corner.

"Dr. Merriweather, can I talk to you for a minute?"

"Certainly, Dr. Eng. Walk with me."

After wishing Michael and Mark luck in their new endeavors, Dr. Merriweather escorts Frank Eng to his office, wondering what he might want to speak about. He's known Eng for a long time and can't tell him anything more about basal cell nevus syndrome that he hasn't discussed in detail before. Originally named Gorlin Syndrome, in honor of Dr. Robert Gorlin, the brilliant oral pathologist from the University of Minnesota who first described it, the syndrome causes its sufferers to repeatedly develop new keratocysts in the jaws. There are other unfortunate effects as part of this syndrome, including skin growths called nevi, pits in the lips and hands, and some abnormal formations of the ribs and skull, all of which Mark and Michael had been spared.

"Nice tie," Frank Eng says as they head down the hall.

"Thanks." Merriweather smiles as he glances down at his printed necktie with the African Big Five on it.

This pleasant reminder of his recent trip stands out

against his usual outfit of slacks, a blue buttoned-down shirt, white physician's coat with ID and security badges hanging from his lapel, and of course the head and neck logo of his specialty.

When they reach his office, Merriweather gestures to a chair and sits behind his desk.

"What can I do for you, Frank?"

Eng reaches into his jacket pocket and withdraws an ornate envelope, which he hands to Merriweather. "Go ahead and open it," he says with a broad smile.

Dr. Merriweather opens the envelope to find an even more ornate invitation to the wedding of Mark Eng to Joy Lee and Michael Eng to Jade lee.

He looks up at Frank in surprise. "The boys are getting married, and to twin sisters? Why, they didn't even mention it in their appointment."

"I asked them to let me tell you and to personally deliver the invitation. So you'll come? I know it's only a little more than three weeks away, and your schedule—"

Dr. Merriweather waves him away. "I wouldn't miss it. Wow, Frank, I'm happy for you. You and Vivian must be very proud."

"We certainly are, Doctor. Now don't go thinking one of the girls is pregnant and this is, how you say, a shotgun wedding. They just want to get married before the boys start working next month."

"I wasn't thinking anything of the sort." Robert smiles.

"In fact, they told me about accepting a job at Ryder. You're lucky again. My own son works there, and I can tell you it's a solid company with good benefits. I'm sure Michael and Mark will go far."

"My family will be honored to have you there. You treated my sons every time they needed it, and you took a special interest in them."

"And I'll be honored to attend, as will my fiancée, Heather."

"Great." A shadow crosses Eng's face. "There's one other thing. It's always worried me, but now with the wedding coming up…"

"What is it, Frank?"

"Will my grandchildren also get this syndrome?"

"Frank, the honest answer is that three out every four will likely, but not necessarily, have this syndrome. While neither you or your wife have shown any signs of it, the gene mutation occurred on its own in the womb and affected both embryos that became Mark and Michael. The inheritance of this mutation is what we call autosomal dominant. That means it can occur in either your granddaughters or grandsons, and it will mostly override their wives' normal gene. But don't despair, Frank. Look how well-adjusted your sons are and what a bright future they have. Their children will have the same."

"Thanks, Doctor. You always tell it like it is and add a note of encouragement." He stands and extends a hand to Dr. Merriweather. "I'll see you at the wedding."

***

On the morning of the wedding, Heather Bellaire steps off the plane at Miami International Airport carrying a light suitcase. As Director of Publications for El Cid Publishing, she usually brings work along with her, but not this time. She's excited about the opportunity to experience a traditional Chinese wedding and to spend more quality time with the man who will soon become her husband. She may even stay a few extra days, for though she has made dozens of trips to Miami over the years, she finds that since becoming engaged, she scrutinizes her future home with new eyes.

Robert and Heather arrive at the temple early. As they take their seats, he explains to her that the wedding procession has actually started hours ago, with the two brides along with their parents and collective bridesmaids arriving by car at the Engs' home. There, according to Mandarin tradition, the bride's procession would be met at the door and formally invited inside. The two brides and their grooms would then each pay their respects to the Jade Emperor, the family's patron deities, deceased ancestors, and on down to their living elders and parents. From there, the brides, grooms, and their parents would proceed to the temple to greet their guests. Then there would be a thirty-minute seating of the guests while the bridal party got prepared. The groom's mother would be seated to the left of the viewing guests, and the groom's father would sit on a slightly elevated platform on the right.

A short while later, Heather and Robert watch, enthralled by the long, bright red silk gowns of the two brides as they stand between Frank and Vivian Eng. They are equally taken aback by the beauty of the brides themselves, with their long, pitch-black hair adorned with jewels and their smooth porcelain skin.

Robert leans in toward Heather. "These boys sure know how to pick 'em," he whispers.

Heather gives Robert a quick smile and touches his hand lightly before turning back to the ceremony unfolding before them. The brides are serving ceremonial tea to their future in-laws when Mark and Michael arrive. They're dressed in bright blue ankle-length robes with black, x-shaped sashes across their chests.

Heather takes in the well-developed physiques of the grooms, which even the robes haven't completely concealed.

"The girls know how to pick 'em too," she retorts with a smile.

The wedding ceremony is followed by a banquet at the elegant Biltmore Hotel in Coral Gables. Called *Xi-Ju*, meaning "joyful wines," the wedding banquet is a lavish affair that usually continues well into the night. The sumptuous ten-course meal begins with a whole traditional shark fin, which Dr. Merriweather politely refuses due to his admiration for the sharks he's encountered while diving and out of respect for their dwindling populations. This is followed with eggs and fish roe to symbolize fertility. Then abalone—a mollusk commonly served at weddings and Chinese New Year—and Hong Kong steak. After the dinner, the brides make their rounds of pouring tea for each guest. Then they and their grooms bow to their guests before adjourning to their honeymoon suites.

After they've gone, the banquet will continue for several more hours, partaking of the delicious fare, mingling, and generally celebrating the happy life that awaits the young couples.

***

An hour later, Mark Eng emerges from the bathroom of his suite, clothed in a full-length red and tan patterned robe. From the bed, Joy, wearing a thin, red nightgown, eyes her new husband appreciatively. They passionately lock eyes, then burst out laughing at the sound of the headboard banging through the wall of the adjacent room.

"It seems that Michael's already ahead of you," Joy murmurs.

Mark faintly hears Jade's encouragement to his brother followed by a squeal of pleasure. He then opens a brown leather pouch containing the powder his father had given both boys before they left the banquet.

"Tonight, you will become men," Frank had announced to them sagely.

As Michael had done earlier, Mark uses a straw to sniff up

a good dose of the powder. He then drops his robe, slowly approaches the bed, and climbs onto his wife, intent on catching up to and surpassing his brother next door. As dutiful and respectful wives, both brides welcome and accept the sexual marathon that continues well into the early morning hours.

***

Back at Dr. Merriweather's home, the atmosphere is much more subdued. Robert, clad only in shorts, lies on his bed proofreading one of his stem cell articles. He's so engrossed in it, and finding too many annoying typos to suit him, that he didn't hear the bathroom door open.

"So," Heather quips saucily, "what does a girl have to do to get noticed around here?"

Robert looks up, his amusement immediately turning to surprise. Heather is standing in the doorway wearing a short, sheer nighty he's never seen before. He silently drinks in her beautiful form, giving particular attention to her dark pink nipples and ample, well-shaped breasts. He then notices the patch of her pubic hair and feels the uncontrollable arousal from within him.

"Well," he says hoarsely as he sets aside the now-unimportant article, "I can see you're not carrying any concealed weapons."

Not to be outdone by Robert's joke, Heather walks up to the end of the bed, one foot in front of the other like a runway model. Smiling seductively, she points to the bulge in Robert's shorts.

"But I can see you're concealing something, aren't you?"

Now it's Robert's turn to smile as Heather, now biting her lower lip, crawls over the bed toward him like a cat on the prowl. After a short but passionate kiss, she straddles him. Not a further word is spoken as she pulls down his shorts and lifts herself to slowly impale herself on the erection. Each lets out a soft moan as Heather slides herself down to the bottom. Then after several minutes of passionate kissing, she begins moving up and down, slow at first, then quickening her pace until, unable to contain themselves any longer, they both explode.

They lay there quietly for several minutes, then Robert asks, "Did the wedding prompt you to do this? Or perhaps it was the thought of a honeymoon?"

"Neither," Heather replies. "It was the thought of you and me spending time together without our work getting in the way, as we did in Africa."

Robert looks at her, one eyebrow raised. "Are you suggesting a move to Miami?"

"Maybe I am."

"Well then, maybe, just maybe, I can live with that."

As Heather drifts off into a blissful sleep, Robert reaches over and plucks the article off the nightstand, thinking he would finish editing it. Instead, he finds himself wrestling with the unanswerable questions that have been plaguing his mind with increasing regularity. Questions like, why couldn't he get his ex-wife out of his mind? Did he love Heather for Heather, or did he just see her as a younger, available version of Veronica? With no answer to those questions, he moves on to some others. Would marriage work for them? For better or worse, they were used to having distance between them. Would they be happy being together all the time? Would Heather be happy moving to Miami? No snow, no colorful leaves in the fall, no Broadway. And the biggest question of all—would his dedication to oral and maxillofacial surgery, his residents, and his research consume him again and drown a marriage to Heather as it did with Veronica?

Robert tosses the article aside again and rubs his eyes wearily. *Heather is beautiful, and she cares for you. She's a catch you can't lose. What're you waiting for, you chump?*

Robert Merriweather, master of human physiology and medicine, admits to himself that he's simply unable to master human emotions and relationships. He finally drifts off to sleep with those troublesome questions still circulating in his mind.

Chapter 15
The Shock

Joy Lee wakes up to a loud banging on the door of her hotel suite. Trying to get the fog of drowsiness out of her eyes, she glances at the clock on the bed stand.

"Good grief, it's already past ten!"

She then glances at her new husband, soundly sleeping on his side with his back turned toward her. As the banging continues, she hears what sounds like the voice of her sister.

"Joy, Mark, come quick!" Jade Lee wails then begins to sob as she renews her banging.

Joy jumps out of bed and runs to the door, barely noticing the soreness in her thigh muscles from the sexual marathon that took place throughout the early morning hours. She whips open the door to find her panic-stricken sister crying and disheveled in a crumpled nightgown. Behind her, a man and woman stand in the doorway of the suite opposite hers, no doubt roused by the commotion. Another man stands a few feet down the hall with a quizzical, worried look on his face.

Now close to hyperventilating, Jade manages to squeak out, "C-come with me. M-Michael's not moving!"

She then grabs Joy's arm and pulls her toward her own suite, with the concerned onlookers following at a distance. When they enter the suite, Joy approaches her new brother-in-law and immediately sees that something is terribly wrong. Michael is lying on his back with his eyes wide open and staring straight ahead.

Joy looks from him to her sister, filled with dreadful foreboding. She then notices the stranger from the hallway standing in the door.

"Let me see him. Maybe I can help," he says as he crosses the room.

The man, who took a CPR course two years ago as a job requirement, immediately notices Michael's pupils are dilated. Not a good sign. He places his fingers on the neck to feel a carotid pulse. Nothing. He then moves to the wrist, trying to feel a radial pulse. Again, no pulse, but he notices the arm to be cooler than he expected.

"Someone call 911!" he shouts then proceeds with the chest compressions he recalls from the course.

The sound of bedsprings squeaking with the rhythmic movement fills the room, followed by the frantic screams of the two brides.

"Call 911—now!" the man repeats between compressions.

He sees the couple standing by the door and jerks his head toward them.

"You—call!"

The man and woman quickly enter the room, the man moving to comfort the girls while the woman pulls out her cell phone to make the call.

"We need help at the Biltmore. A man's not breathing. Hurry, please!"

It occurs to Joy Lee that Mark isn't there, that he hadn't been woken up as she had by her sister's banging. A new fear rising within her, she tears herself away from her sister and rushes toward her own suite. The man consoling her leaves his wife to attend to Jade Lee and follows. The two push past several other hotel guests gathering in the hallway. Joy rushes to Mark's side and turns him over on his back. She gasps in horror when she sees the same wide-eyed stare.

"Mark, Mark." She roughly grips his shoulders. "Wake up, wake up, please wake up!"

No response.

The man pulls out his cell phone and makes another call to 911.

"Yes," he says breathlessly, "I'm calling from the Biltmore. There's another man here not breathing!" He then runs out into the crowded hallway and shouts, "Does anyone here know CPR?"

Within minutes, several hotel supervisors and security guards arrive at the scene, followed closely by the EMTs responding to the 911 calls. The team splits up, with one member relieving the man administering CPR to Michael, and the other beginning to work on Mark. However, just a few minutes later, they both return to the hallway, their faces solemn. Both young men have died. The realization that their new husbands are gone, and with them, their plans for the future, hits both brides like a runaway truck. Jade passes out, and Joy becomes so overwrought that the EMTs must give her a sedative.

Thirty minutes later, Frank Eng arrives at the hotel after receiving a cryptic phone call from one of the hotel supervisors. When he reaches the floor where the honeymoon suites are located, he's shocked to see his two daughters-in-law sitting on the hallway floor with their backs against a wall. Both are sobbing.

"Joy? Jade Lee?" He rushes over to them. "What's the matter? They called and told me to come here. Said there was some sort of trouble?"

They look up at him, their eyes glazed over with shock. That's when he notices the police officers standing at the entrances of the suites. With a sinking feeling in his stomach, he hurries over to them.

"I'm the father of the men staying in these suites, and I want to see them right now."

"Sorry, sir, but no one is allowed in the suites right now."

Desperate, Frank tries to push his way past them but finds himself held in place by the officer's steely grip.

"I demand that you let me in!" he yells.

A moment later, the door to Michael and Jade's suite opens, and a man wearing a suit and a detective's shield around his neck steps into the hall. Then, with real sympathy in his eyes, the detective delivers the news that no parent should ever hear. Frank Eng emits a sharp scream of agony then feels the cop's arms go around him as he collapses to the floor.

***

"At least he died happy," another, coarser detective quips as he looks down at Mark's body.

"Very funny," the other detective replies.

The detective made the same joke while in Michael's room and noted that the Eng brother had also died with an erection. The cops had also been quick to note the near-empty pouches of gray powder in each room and that some of the dust was present around the nostrils of the deceased.

One of the detectives advances a preliminary diagnosis. "Looks like snorting a little coke isn't good for a long-term marriage."

"I dunno," another replies, "it's grayer and finer than cocaine, and it doesn't clump together like cocaine does. Then again, it could be a synthetic or new formula, or just another bad batch from Mexico."

A few hours later, the CSI team has finished taking

pictures of the scene and bagging the evidence, including the leather pouches, a glass of half-drunk wine, and even the bed sheets. Outside, the hallways have been cleared of onlookers, and Joy, Jade, and Frank Eng have been led away by grief counselors, spared the sight of their loved ones being placed on stretchers and carted off to the medical examiner's office.

Chapter 16
The Autopsy

On the Monday morning following the wedding, the four newlyweds were supposed to be enjoying a lovely late breakfast with their parents before embarking on a short but fun-filled Caribbean honeymoon cruise. Instead, the widows and their families are planning funerals while the lifeless bodies of Mark and Michael lay on adjacent, cold, stainless steel autopsy tables, covered with clean white sheets. At the foot of the tables stands a disbelieving Dr. Merriweather.

Though he hasn't been involved with an autopsy since his residency days, Dr. Merriweather is planning to assist Dr. Joseph Wright, Director of the Medical Examiner's Office. Frank Eng had personally asked him to be present, and Robert gladly rearranged his schedule in the hopes that it would help alleviate some of his friend's grief.

Dreading the gruesome task, Merriweather is somewhat comforted by knowing that he'll be working with the venerable Dr. Wright. The sixty-eight year old with thinning, gray hair has performed thousands of forensic autopsies and testified in numerous murder trials over his thirty-four-year career. He's a by-the-book medical examiner who records every detail and leaves nothing unexplored.

A forensic autopsy doesn't start with bodily incisions, as depicted on TV and in films, but with photographs, X-rays, and a thorough topographical examination of the entire body surface, including every orifice. As they begin, Dr. Merriweather is immediately put at ease by Joe's welcoming demeanor. He'd been concerned that his presence may be taken as an intrusion or annoyance. Instead, the medical examiner seems to enjoy having Robert at his side and treats him like a student, pointing out details as he goes.

With the preliminaries done, Doctors Wright and Merriweather put on barrier gowns, gloves, caps, and masks with shields to prevent splatter to their faces, as is done in every operating room on a live patient. Dr. Wright then turns to the body of Mark Eng and begins making the traditional Y-shaped incision of an autopsy. The two arms of the Y cross Mark's chest, from just short of each shoulder, and meet at the tip of the sternum. This is known as the xiphoid process. Wright follows with the straight stem of the Y, cutting down the abdomen to the just above the genitalia to open up the chest and abdominal cavities. He then takes a heavy bolt cutter to cut the breast bone up to the clavicle so he can access the heart and lungs. It's at that point where many medical students faint or excuse themselves for the remainder of the autopsy. The two experienced and battle-hardened doctors are unfazed. Though several times, Robert finds himself forcing the agonized face of Frank Eng from his mind.

Merriweather and Wright now proceed to remove every internal organ, weigh it, catalog it, and take a piece for microscopic analysis. After peeling the scalp back, Dr. Wright hands a surprised Dr. Merriweather the rotary saw needed to cut the top of the skull.

"You didn't think I was going to do all the work, did you, Bobby? I hear you're an expert at cutting bone. Go for it."

With a nod, Merriweather obliges and cuts the skull cap off just above the level of the ears. He then assists Dr. Wright in removing the brain and taking samples from various areas known for specific functions.

The remainder of the autopsy is concluded with the taking of blood samples from the large vessels. It's only then, as he watches Wright turn the faucet and sees Mark Eng's blood flow down the tapered autopsy table to the drain, that he allows the full import of what he's done overtake him. The blood was the same he'd seen during the seven surgeries he performed on the young man over the course of fifteen years. Never, in all those times, had he ever imagined he'd be seeing it under these circumstances, or Mark's lifeless body devoid of its internal organs. He can only shake his head and try to imagine how this family will ever be able to cope with such a tragedy.

He hears Dr. Wright clear his throat, a gentle reminder that their work isn't over.

"Didn't see much," Wright says. "No evidence of pathology. Just some rib abnormalities and some barely noticeable pits on the palms of his hands, consistent with the basal cell nevus syndrome you told me about. Nothing that would jump out at you as the cause of death. But I suspect that powder the cops found at their bedsides will be revealing. It's being tested now. I'll also have the blood samples tested by gas-liquid chromatography to see if that powdered stuff was in their systems." Wright turns to the body of Michael Eng. "Now, let's see about the brother."

After completing the second autopsy in the same manner, the two adjourn to Joe Wright's office down the hall. On the way, they grab soft drinks from the vending machine—a Diet Coke for Joe, and a Diet Dr. Pepper for Dr. Merriweather. It's his favorite form of sustenance on the best of days, and he finds that he's in desperate need of it now.

They arrive at the office to find the report of the chemical analysis of the mysterious powder already on Joe's desk.

"Can't beat the Dade County M.E.'s office." Joe begins pouring over the report.

Sipping his Dr. Pepper, Robert walks behind him and reads over his shoulder.

"Holy shit!" Wright exclaims. "It's keratin and sildenafil." He looks up at Robert. "What are two twenty-one year olds doing snorting Viagra, and what the hell is the purpose of the keratin?"

"I don't believe it," Robert says slowly as realization dawns.

"Don't believe what?"

"Two months ago, I went on a photographic safari at Simbambili Lodge in South Africa. The staff there told us that rhino poachers have been more active than ever, and—"

"Wait a minute, Bob. What do rhinos have to do with any of this?"

"In China, many grooms use powdered rhino horn on their wedding night with the belief that it will increase their libido and stamina."

"Oh, geez...."

"Yes, and the poachers have been adding Viagra to the ground-up rhino horn to add credibility to its lore as a sexual performance enhancer. We even came upon some poachers who had been mauled by two lions. Two of them were killed and partly eaten, but we managed to save the third one. Quite an effort, I assure you. Anyway, the addition of Viagra has sent the demand for powdered rhino horn soaring, not only in China but numerous other Southeast Asian countries. Poaching, I'm afraid, has increased in kind, to the point that the white rhino is on the brink of extinction."

"Well, I'll be dammed." Joe looks back down at the report. "There's one other ingredient in this mixture— one that isn't in our profile. What's that doing in there? Any mention of some mystery drug from the guides at Simbambili?"

"No, they couldn't even attest to the Viagra. It was only a well-circulated rumor."

"Well, it's not a rumor anymore. But I'll need time to find out what this X factor is."

Just then, a technician enters the office and hands Joe the printed blood sample report. "You know the old phrase, 'I love you to death'?" he says. "That's what this reads like."

Ignoring the remark, the two doctors scan the report, which is in the form of a graph. They immediately focus on one of two large spikes on the graph. The technician marked one as sildenafil, or Viagra, and the other as UNK, for unknown.

"Bob, these kids have a massive overdose of Viagra in their blood, about ten times more than the dose they would get from the little blue pill. They died of hypotension, leading to cardiac arrest. No wonder we didn't find any real pathology. I'll bet their blood pressure went all the way down to zero with this much in their system." Joe looks at Dr. Merriweather with an unblinking stare. "I suppose you've seen the Viagra commercials warning potential buyers not to use Viagra with nitrates or blood-pressure-lowering medicines for fear of lowering their blood pressure to dangerously low levels. Well, the same thing has happened here, and to a much greater degree."

"Do you think this extra compound in the powder is a nitrate?"

"If it is, it's not one in our battery of tests. The problem is that now I'll have to sign this out as a homicide."

This revelation stuns Dr. Merriweather as he tries to figure out how he's going to explain this to Dr. Eng and his wife.

It doesn't take long for that challenge to confront him. After leaving Joe's office, he checks his phone and finds two messages from Frank Eng asking for updates on the M.E.'s report.

"Might as well get this over with," Robert mutters.

He calls Frank back and asks him to come to Dr. Wright's office. He's not surprised when, just three minutes later, Frank walks in, followed by his wife, Vivian.

"She insisted on coming," Frank whispers.

"I understand," Robert replies gently, though he hoped to speak about this delicate matter with Frank alone.

He gestures for them to take a seat and explains that the powdered rhino horn contained some poison that was inadvertently incorporated into it. He thought the little white lie might soften the blow. He was wrong.

When he hears the news, Frank Eng's eyes widen, and the color drains from his face. Beside him, his wife gasps and dissolves into quiet sobs.

"I—I gave them the pouches," Frank whispers. "I didn't know. It was something we're supposed to do. I used it on my own wedding night, as did my father and my grandfather on theirs."

"Frank, where did you get this stuff?"

"In Chicago, two weeks ago. I was there for the Society of Chemical Engineer's Meeting. I went to a Chinese cultural medicine store, one I've been to before. They sell all the different Chinese herbal medicines and do acupuncture as well. They're very respected in the neighborhood. I would've never thought...."

At a loss for words, Merriweather looks on helplessly as he, too, begins to sob.

CHAPTER 17
Goliath's Revenge
and the Big Tuskers

About the same time as the unfortunate demise of the two young Chinese grooms, the cargo ship *Dragon Master* pulls into Hong Kong Harbor. In anticipation of its arrival, Tang Ma, the biggest ivory distributor in all of China, has bribed the local dock hands to unload his cargo first and without asking questions. Tang Ma has anxiously awaited the arrival of this cargo for the past three weeks as the *Dragon Master* made its seven-thousand-mile voyage from Mombasa to Hong Kong. He has a long list of well-to-do local clients who want ivory chopsticks and earrings, as well as Western knives and forks with ivory handles. He's also reconnected with previous clients in Europe and the United States who want distinctive ivory ornaments and other applications. Over the years, Tang Ma has earned the reputation of being willing to ship anything to anyone, anywhere, regardless of the legality or human cost.

At 6:00 a.m. the next morning, one hundred ninety-seven girls—mostly from poor rural families and between the ages of nine and seventeen—file into Tang Ma's factory. Tang prefers to employ young girls, as they possess the small hands and fine motor skills needed to work the hard ivory tusks into the various detailed ornaments. And poor ones, as they're more likely to please him in other ways in the hopes of gaining special privileges.

The space is an old, dilapidated warehouse without windows, heating, or air conditioning. Large fans sit in each corner, but given the size of the space, they have little effect on the temperature during warmer months. During the winter, the girls are expected to wear coats but no gloves so as to keep their hands nimble and working quickly. There are twelve workstations in a row, each illuminated by a single light bulb hanging from a cord that stretches the length of the row. The girls' workday begins the moment they arrive and continues until 7:00 p.m., with only short breaks for lunch and dinner. The young women eat at their workstations, hurriedly consuming whatever food they've brought over from the dormitory or from their own homes so they can meet their quota and not lose part of their already meager salary.

At one such workstation, fourteen-year-old Li Chi is given a six-inch cut of a tusk and a rectangular metal piece. A two-year veteran at Tang Ma's factory, she has the precise eye-hand coordination of a jeweler. She knows that a groove must be made in the flat end to receive the stub of the rectangular metal piece, and that her more demanding task will be to carve out small images of elephants, lions, leopards, Cape buffalo and rhinoceros, known as the Big Five. She doesn't know, however, that she's making a bottle opener destined for some department store in the United States, or that the Big Five was so named because they were the five most dangerous and therefore sought after trophies by the great white hunters at the beginning of the last century.

As she plods through the squalid factory, day after day, Li Chi focuses on her only goal—to save up enough money to someday move to Beijing, where her older sister has a restaurant. Li Chi can work for better pay and fewer hours. After two years, however, she has nowhere near what she needs to leave. In her lowest moments, she contemplates selling her virginity to Tang Ma, but one look at the loathsome man and she knows she can't go through with it. At least, not yet.

***

One week after the autopsies of Mark and Michael Eng, Dr. Merriweather is back at his clinic, seeing patients and teaching his residents and fellows in oral and maxillofacial tumor and reconstructive surgery. His busy clinic is interrupted by a phone call from his secretary, Michelle Ruiz.

"Chief, there is a Dr. Wendell on the phone for you. Do you want to take the call?"

"Mishy, transfer Dr. Wendell to my office. I'll take it there."

Dr. Merriweather knows Dr. Jane Wendell, the most prominent dermatologist in South Florida, very well. They have shared numerous patients in the past as well as a keen interest in skin healing promotions using stem cells and growth factor therapy, known as Platelet Rich Plasma, or PRP, which Dr. Merriweather introduced to medicine.

"Jane, nice to hear from you. What's up?"

"I know it's your busy clinic day, but I have a man in my office who has a concerning black ulcer on his forehead. I think it might be skin cancer. Can you squeeze him in today?"

"Of course, Jane. One more won't make a big difference. Have him come to our clinic around five. We should be winding down by then."

"Thanks, Bob. I really appreciate you doing this."

Indeed, by 5:00 p.m., the clinic patients have all been seen, and the man referred by Dr. Wendell has already been interviewed by Dr. Merriweather's fellow Dr. Ledoux. When he enters the room, Dr. Merriweather is taken aback by the sheer size and presence of the man, who is six-foot-four and heavily muscled. He's also quick to note the one-inch, oval-shaped black ulcer on his forehead surrounded by a rim of mildly swollen, red skin.

"Hello there, I'm Dr. Merriweather. I see you've already met my right-hand man, Dr. Ledoux. He's going to tell me a little about you. Then I'll see what I can do to help you, okay?"

"Okay, mate. Dr. Wendell said you're the best."

Dr. Merriweather nods and turns to his fellow. "Dr. Ledoux, what have you learned from this gentleman?"

"Dr. Merriweather, this is Mr. James McCullar. He's forty-two years old and, as you can tell from the accent, originally from Australia. Though, he travels a great deal. He's here on vacation and went to see Dr. Wendell about the ulcer on his forehead, to the left of the midline, that showed up about six days ago. He says it isn't painful, but it's increased in size. His past medical history is essentially free of any medical conditions. He's had a few old fractures that have completely healed, and apparently two superficial bullet wounds, but no serious injuries."

As Dr. Ledoux launches into his examination findings, Dr. Merriweather interrupts him and dons a pair of blue plastic gloves.

"Mr. McCullar, I see the edge of another ulcer through the sleeve opening of your shirt. Would you mind taking your shirt off for me?"

Jim McCullar removes his shirt to reveal two smaller but similar black ulcers on his left wrist, and another two even smaller ones on the finger pads of his right hand.

"Mr. McCullar, I suspect you're right-handed. Are you?"

"Sure, mate, but I'm not bad with my left one either."

Dr. Merriweather now takes a look at the forehead ulcer and notices a slight wince from the macho Australian when he presses on it. A small amount of pus also exudes from around the edges of the ulcer.

"Is it cancer, Doc? If it is, I want you to remove it ASAP."

"Mr. McCullar, most skin cancers are caused by long-term sun exposure, which I gather you've had. However, the pattern of your other ulcers places most of them in areas you cover up, particularly the finger pads of your right hand. I suspect these ulcers are some form of an infection that you've spread from your right hand to your left wrist and to the left side of your forehead. Do you ever find yourself wiping sweat off your forehead while you're working outdoors?"

"Sure, all the time. Is this one of those sex diseases? Big Jim is popular with the ladies, you know."

"It could be, Mr. McCullar. We'll need to do some blood tests and take a biopsy and culture sample of one of the lesions to pinpoint it. You put your shirt back on, and I'll numb the area on your forehead with a little local anesthetic. Then I'll take a small sample and draw a few blood samples."

Jim McCullar visibly recoils at the suggestion. "Oh no, Doc, me and needles don't get along very well."

"Mr. McCullar, certainly a big man like you can take two little needle pinches to numb up your skin. There's really no way we can do it without them."

With a reluctant nod, Big Jim McCullar closes his eyes and commences kicking and wincing.

"I haven't even started yet, Mr. McCullar," Dr. Merriweather says. "You can relax for a few minutes while I get everything ready. I'll let you know before I pinch you with the needle, okay?"

"Okay, Doc."

Then he employs an old trick used by nearly every dentist

and some physicians as well. He presses the skin while explaining that he wants to check the ulcer one more time. While doing so, he inserts the needle under the skin where he presses the hardest and slowly injects the local anesthetic.

"Okay, Mr. McCullar, are you ready?"

With that, Big Jim grabs the chair handles with a white-knuckled grip and tightens his big muscles in anticipation of the worst to come.

"Okay, Doc, give me the needles."

Merriweather grins. "Actually, Mr. McCullar, we've already injected the local anesthetic. Been done for several minutes."

Big Jim signs in relief. "You did? I didn't even feel it. Dr. Wendell said you're the best."

Dr. Merriweather and Dr. Ledoux trade a wry smile between them, then go about the task of collecting a small but sufficiently sized sample of the ulcer. They do so with a horizontal incision that will allow the resulting scar to blend into a natural skin fold.

Dr. Merriweather instructs his fellow to also submit a small piece of the specimen for bacteria staining and for culture. He then proceeds to draw two blood samples, but not before anesthetizing the skin with a refrigerant.

"Thanks, mate," Big Jim says. "Now fix me up. Big Jim's got some serious partying to do."

CHAPTER 18
Straight Talk

Three days after Jim McCullar's biopsy and cultures, Dr. Merriweather gets a call to come to the office of Dade South Hospital's CEO, Yvonne Diaz. As he washes up after his morning surgery, Merriweather wonders what's on Yvonne's mind. She's usually supportive of the physician staff and not overbearing with regard to the plethora of regulations imposed on hospitals today. In fact, Dr. Merriweather has always respected her straight-shooter approach and considers her a friend. Nevertheless, as he walks over to the administration area, he wonders what this is all about. Another Joint Commission Inspection? Did one of his residents utter an insensitive remark to a nurse or patient? Is there some new language the government requires on the consent form of the awful and useless HIPAA regulations? A myriad of possibilities. He resigns himself to just wait and find out.

Upon arrival at her office, he's greeted by two other longtime colleagues and friends—Dr. Rebecca Palmer, General Pathologist and Director of the Lab, and Dr. Raj Chandra, an infectious disease specialist. Rebecca is a trim, attractive blonde, and Raj, though a bit too thin, has bronze skin and thick black hair. Like Merriweather, both are in their mid-fifties but look several years younger.

"Rebecca, Raj, nice to see you. Are you part of this meeting?"

They nod, but before they can elaborate, Yvonne Diaz breaks in. "Let me get right to the point. Dr. Palmer has identified anthrax on the culture of one of your patients, a Mr. Jim McCullar. What do you know about him?"

"Anthrax, really? I had suspected an infection, but not anthrax. As for McCullar, seems he's some type of mercenary soldier. I know he's been to Africa and the Middle East, and now he's tearing through the clubs and party scenes on Miami Beach."

Yvonne nods. "Okay, well Rebecca says this is some kind of altered anthrax bacillus. She's not able to pinpoint the alteration, but we may be dealing with a weaponized anthrax, possibly a totally resistant strain. Or worse, much more contagious. We don't want any word of this leaking out, but the CDC protocols require us to send them a sample and quarantine the patient. Rebecca, have you sent the samples off to the CDC yet?"

"They went out this morning right after your call. Thank goodness there was enough left to send. I sent them to the attention of Peter Fowler. He's in charge of communicable diseases."

Shocked by this turn of events, Dr. Merriweather turns to Raj. "Raj, if we don't have antibiotic sensitivities yet, how should we treat this guy initially?"

"Since we have nothing to go on, I would start treating

him with either one of the two anthrax standards—ciprofloxacin or doxycycline, or both. But we should get chest and abdominal CT scans. Cutaneous anthrax is curable if it's not a resistant strain. However, pulmonary and abdominal anthrax can be deadly from any anthrax bacillus. It's what the weaponized anthrax developed by the old Soviet Union targeted, and was revealed when the medical files were inspected after the Berlin Wall came down."

Dr. Chandra proceeds to tell the group of the identified stores of super bacteria, mostly anthrax, developed and stored in the old Soviet Union during the height of the Cold War. Some stores of anthrax couldn't be accounted for and are suspected to still be stored away somewhere in Russia or Iran.

"Well, that's scary," Yvonne replies. "And that's why we need to keep this quiet. Quarantine this guy, and get his treatment started. Raj, you and I will talk to him when he comes in. Robert, bring him up to the third-floor VIP suite. We'll house him there. I'll get security to stand guard over the room."

"He's due to see me at three today," Merriweather says. "I'll be glad to bring him up there. But I warn you, this guy is big and strong and not the most compliant person I've seen with regard medical issues. Use your biggest security guards, your most persuasive language, and don't talk to him in medical terms. He'll just shut you out."

"Understood," Yvonne says. "I've done this before and am actually very good at it. I'm sure Raj and I can make him understand."

An hour after, Dr. Merriweather brought Big Jim McCullar to the third-floor VIP suite, with a brief explanation about anthrax and the necessity of treating it, as well as registering a concern about the new black crusting sore on his face and several more on his arms. He's now lecturing to his residents on several tumor types and how they should be treated. His attention is drawn to an overhead page in a panicky tone, asking him to return to the third-floor suite, STAT.

After muttering an apology about cutting his lecture short, Merriweather rushes out of the room and up the staircase, to the third floor, fearful of a medical emergency. Instead, he sees his patient has one of the security guards in a stranglehold. A second guard is off to the side with a bloody lip and several missing teeth, being attended to by one of the nursing staff. A disheveled Yvonne Diaz rushes up to him.

"Please, Bob, talk to him before he hurts someone else. I've already called the police, but we still need to quarantine him. Maybe you can get through to him."

Merriweather nods and turns to the enraged Australian. "Mr. McCullar, let our security guard go. He's no threat to an experienced soldier like you."

McCullar narrows his eyes at him, and for a moment Merriweather thinks he's only made things worse. Then the Australian shrugs.

"Yeah, you're right, Doc." He releases the guard, who falls to the floor and quickly scrambles to his feet and out the door of Big Jim's room. "But these blighters want to lock me up and do medical experiments on me. Not on Big Jim McCullar they won't."

"Mr. McCullar, no one is going to experiment on you. Now close the door and sit down."

"No way, mate. Big Jim is leaving right now."

Seeing logic is getting him nowhere, Merriweather takes a different tact. "Mr. McCullar, sit your dumb ass down right now!"

Big Jim moves toward Dr. Merriweather with a combined look of anger and bewilderment. No one since his abusive father had ever talked to him in such a tone and got away with anything less than a painful beating.

Instead of cowering, as most would under the threatening glare, Dr. Merriweather merely crosses his arms across his chest.

"No one talks to Big Jim like that. No one!"

In a loud voice, Dr. Merriweather responds, "Well, I am, Mr. McCullar, because I'm trying to save your damn life. Now sit down, shut up, and listen to me!"

Big Jim is taken aback by the implied threat to his life and the continued bravado of Dr. Merriweather. However, he's no longer on the plains or in the jungles of Africa or the desert sands of the Middle East, but in an unfamiliar jungle called a hospital, where all the 9mm's and knives in the world can't save him. Here, Dr. Merriweather, with his dress shirt, necktie, and white lab coat with several medical ID badges hanging from the lapels, is the alpha male.

McCullar sits.

"Now," Merriweather exhales as he sits across from him, "you came to Miami Beach to party and get as much … pussy … um … as many ladies as you can, right?"

"Yeah, you got that right." McCullar sniffs, glad the conversation has shifted back to a topic he's comfortable with. "And Big Jim doesn't need to try for it, either. The Sheilas come to me."

"Well, I'll wager you haven't been as popular with the Sheilas since you developed those ugly, black, crusty sores, now have you?"

"I still do okay."

"Jim, I don't think you're doing as okay as you say. Remember, I'm a guy, too. Now think how well you're going to do when your entire face is covered by these sores. No Sheila is even going to want to look at you, let alone touch you."

"You mean, it's gonna to get worse?"

"Yes, a lot worse. You're going to get uglier, and then you'll die. Plain and simple. These people and I are trying to save your damn life, but we need you to help us. Stay put and get the treatment you need here, and then guess what'll happen?"

"What, Doc?"

"The black sores will heal and go away. You'll then look as good to the ladies as before. You can go back to Miami Beach and get in all the action you want. Sound good?"

Jim takes a moment to consider his words. "Okay, Doc, but as soon as these black sores heal, I'm outta here. Deal?"

"A deal is a deal, Mr. McCullar," replies Dr. Merriweather, unaware that he's using Big Jim's own expression.

Jim grins, and as Robert leaves the room, the mercenary is already lying in bed and flipping through the sports channels.

Outside the room, he finds that the hospital staff has returned to their regular routine as if the earlier commotion never occurred. Not so for Yvonne Diaz and Dr. Chandra, however, who still look unnerved.

"He agreed to the quarantine?" Dr. Chandra asked.

"Yes, he did, after some bluffing on my part. Not at all sure I can deliver on what I promised."

"The important thing is that you got him to agree," Yvonne says.

"We should start him on Ciprofloxacin, 750 milligrams, twice a day," Dr. Raj says. "And we should take it ourselves as a precaution."

"How'd you do it?" Yvonne asks, incredulously.

Robert shrugs. "Easy—I speak Australian."

CHAPTER 19
Frustration and Depression

The next morning, Dr. Merriweather wakes up to a voicemail from Dr. Joe Wright. He returns the call as he's driving to the hospital, hoping the medical examiner has more news about the rhino powder that killed the two Eng boys.

"Yes, Joe, I got your message. You have news for me?"

"Sure do. That unknown stuff is an enzyme. And a completely new one, at that. It interferes with the metabolism of the sildenafil to make it more potent and last longer. It's actually the agent that caused the Viagra to kill those two boys."

"What the hell was that doing in a bag of rhino horn powder and Viagra? Was it contamination?"

"Not at all. Whoever put it in there was very sophisticated and knew exactly what they were doing. They actually bound the enzyme to the Viagra with a weak electrical charge so that every molecule of Viagra would be attached to it. The ratios were equal and constant." Wright sighs. "Bob, those boys didn't have a chance."

Once again, the vision of the sobbing Frank and Vivian Eng flashes through Robert's mind. "That's terrible, Joe."

"And that's not all. When I gave our data sheets to the FBI, I learned that rhino-horn-powder-related deaths have become an epidemic. Interpol may get involved. It seems the Engs were among the first, but they certainly won't be the last."

"But who's behind all this?" Robert asks, more to himself than to Wright.

The whole dirty business reminds him of something North Star or Apollo would do. He quickly dismisses the thought as ridiculous and a result of his loathing of the two pharmaceutical giants. Though it has been a few years, Robert remembers like yesterday his court battles with North Star and Apollo over the effects of their drugs on osteoporosis and cancer patients. Both companies had a track record for a willingness to do anything to increase their bottom line, no matter the cost to human life.

✳✳✳

That same morning, Frank Eng takes the early American Airlines flight from Miami to Chicago. When he arrives at O'Hare, he takes a cab to a small shop a block from the intersection of Wentworth and Archer Streets, in the middle of Chinatown. As he quietly meanders through the aisles, he smells a faint but pungent odor he recognizes as that of dead animal bones. Indeed, the aisles are filled with musty bins containing various animal bones, skins, and claws, each marked with the ailment its contents are used to treat. Stomachaches, headaches, menstrual pain, joint pain, and so on. He then sees the numerous jars of powdered somethings or ointments and various creams on an old shelf behind the counter, also labeled for its use to treat a specific ailment.

Frank Eng notes that the store is quiet today, nothing like the beehive of activity he's seen on previous occasions. He also notices that some of the bins that were once full are now empty, as are several shelves.

He gradually makes his way to the clerk and asks to speak to the owner. This is the protocol for getting something that can't be displayed in the open. The clerk nods curtly then disappears into a back room. A moment later, he's replaced by a Mr. Huang Lee, the same person who sold him the rhino horn powder that killed his two sons.

With a respectful bow, Frank Eng tells him he would like to purchase rhino horn powder. He plans to test it for the poisons that killed his sons.

"We don't sell rhino horn powder," Lee indignantly retorts. "It's illegal. We are a legal establishment."

"Mr. Lee, you sold me rhino horn powder just two months ago."

"You are mistaken. We never sell rhino horn powder. You must've bought it somewhere else."

Now, with a raised and agitated voice, Frank says, "No! I bought it right here, from you, in this very room. You can't deny it. My sons died from it. You murdered them."

At the word "murder," the store's only other two customers stop in their tracks and look over. Huang Lee's eyes widen, and for a moment, he looks afraid. He then glances toward the back room and calls out, "Dan, Jack, take this crazy man out of here!"

Huang's two strapping sons come out of the backroom, grab Frank Eng by the shoulders, and drag him out to the curb kicking and screaming. But when he threatens Huang Lee personally, Jack Lee, the bigger of the two, responds by raining several punches to Frank's face, resulting in three loosened upper teeth and a bloody nose. They leave him in a disheveled heap on the curb next to a metal meshed city waste container.

In pain and out of options, Frank Eng bows his battered head, closes his eyes, and allows the waves of grief and shame to wash over him. He finds just enough energy to pick himself up and head back to the airport and then home to begin a downward spiral of depression.

CHAPTER 20
A Different Type of Predator

On a Friday night, just four days after his release from a one-week quarantine, Big Jim sits on a barstool at the Crystal Palace Club in Miami Beach. Just one week of treatment has healed all his cutaneous anthrax sores, leaving only a small scar on his forehead, which only adds to his rugged charm. It's just this charm, combined with his obvious physical strength and stories of adventures in the outback and Africa, that has enthralled his two young female companions.

Jane and Joanie, both nineteen and roommates at a local college, are just two of the thousands of coeds shirking their studies to partake of the South Beach nightlife. Veterans of college bars, they've tired of the weak pickup lines of immature young men and are completely taken in by the handsome outdoorsman with an Australian accent and wild tales. This isn't just some frat boy looking to get laid or a nerd with his head buried in books. He's a real man who has really lived. They don't know how the evening will progress or which one of them he'll choose, but they're willing to find out. Against the backdrop of flashing lights, dance music, and scantily-dressed, beautiful people, they look at him, starry-eyed and ask him to tell yet another story.

Unbeknownst to Jane and Joanie, they have other competition for Big Jim's affections. Observing them from the other end of the bar is Marilyn Wasniewski, a drop-dead gorgeous blond known locally as Marilyn Waters. Born and raised in the Bronx, she grew up fast after an unplanned pregnancy and a subsequent abortion at the age of fifteen. It was then that her mother, who had also been around the block at an early age, imparted the advice Marilyn has followed ever since. Boys think you're pretty and want you. String them along, flatter them, give them just enough to want more, and make them pay for everything they get.

Now, at age thirty-three, she's the most desirable call girl in Miami. And at five thousand a night, one of the most highly paid. She has a group of regulars, usually older businessmen, politicians, and local media personnel, who are more than happy to pay her fee, knowing that it includes Marilyn's absolute discretion. When not with one of her regulars, she and her business partner Dante can be found combing the city's finer establishments for a rich mark, and as the saying goes, roll him for his dough. She met the short Cuban-American at a party a few years ago, and the two have enjoyed a profitable arrangement ever since.

"Dante, we got a live one over there." She gives a subtle nod toward Big Jim, who at that moment is peeling a hundred off a sizable roll of cash.

"Oh, I spotted him a while ago and heard him, too, even over the noise in here. You, sweetheart, need to get him away from those little fools and outside so I can introduce him to Mr. Smith and Mr. Wesson."

As Dante laughs at his own joke, Marilyn sizes up the two wide-eyed coeds with their too-tight, mid-thigh-length dresses.

"Not so fast, Dante. I want to have some fun first." Marilyn's eyes flick over Big Jim, taking in the size of his biceps as he flexes for the girls. Most of her clients are old guys who collapse on top of her within ten minutes flat. This one looks like he could go all night and then some.

"Let this lioness play with the King of the Jungle over there before you come in."

"Okay, okay, have your fun. But I'll be at your apartment before dawn. Just get him ready."

Contrasted to the two coeds, Marilyn wears a mid-calf red dress with a slit up one side, a neat white blouse, tasteful diamond earrings, and a blue pearl necklace. She projects the image of a refined lady. She slowly walks up to the threesome and insinuates herself between Big Jim and the two girls.

Then, adopting an apologetic expression, she says, "Ladies, can I interrupt you for a moment? I need to talk to my boyfriend here."

With the girls already forgotten, Marilyn turns toward Big Jim with a knowing smile. Behind her, Jane and Joanie exchange confused glances then slip off their stools and fade into the crowd of gyrating bodies. Big Jim matches Marilyn's smile with one of his own.

"You are my boyfriend, aren't you?" Marilyn says.

"Lady, I can be whatever you want me to be." Big Jim chuckles. "At least for tonight. Can I buy you a drink?"

Neither are in a rush. Like most experienced players, they like to savor the game before claiming their prize. After an hour of drinks, a few of Big Jim's real-life stories, and a few of Marilyn's made-up ones, she suggests they move the party to her place. Big Jim pulls out a few more hundreds to settle the bill while Marilyn texts the driver she employs on such occasions to meet her at the entrance.

As he slips into the waiting limo, Big Jim asks, "Just how much is this little party going to cost me?"

Marilyn draws back in mock surprise at his insinuation and laughs. "This one's on me."

"Really?" Big Jim replies with a raised eyebrow.

He's been offered a freebie or two, but never by such a beautiful and classy lady as this.

"Really."

"Okay, but I'm gonna hold you to this. A deal is a deal, right?"

The foreplay begins even before the limo pulls up to the apartment building on Brickell Avenue. When they arrive, Jim slips out first and offers a hand to help Marilyn out of the car. Then, with his big arm wrapped around her shoulder, they head into the building. Once in the elevator, Marilyn presses the button for the twenty-seventh floor and reaches up to place her lips on his neck and a hand on his muscular chest.

As the elevator doors open to the penthouse floor, Marilyn pulls away and reaches in her purse for her keys and waves them at him seductively. As he enters, Big Jim immediately notices the big, round bed adorned with satin sheets. Behind it is a large sliding glass door leading out to a spacious balcony. The smell of the apartment is an enticing mixture of apple blossom and apricot. Marilyn goes straight to a well-stocked cherrywood bar and sets two glasses on it.

"What's your pleasure, Big Jim?"

"You're my pleasure, lady. But if you're talking about a drink, I'll take Crown Royal on the rocks."

"Well, Jim, we think alike. Go out on the balcony, and I'll join you in a minute."

Jim steps outside and inhales contentedly. Marilyn Water's balcony overlooks Biscayne Bay and Key Biscayne. The view is breathtaking and romantic, with the lights of small boats and yachts cruising the intercostal waterway between the mainland and Key Biscayne, as well as the lights from Key Biscayne itself.

A moment later, he hears Marilyn's heels as she steps onto the balcony, then feels her arms reach around his waist. A few minutes later, they lay on the large, round bed, leaving the ice in their untouched drinks to melt in the humid Miami night.

***

Six hours of sexual Olympics later, the two are sleeping soundly between the crumpled satin sheets. Outside by the elevator, Dante runs a hand over his stubbly beard. He has been there for over an hour and is tired of waiting. Surely, Marilyn's had her fill by now.

He removes his shoes, quietly unlocks the door, and slips inside the apartment. He gives himself a few minutes to allow his eyes to adjust to the darkness, then he observes the scene before him. The Australian is laying on his right side while Marilyn lies facedown to his left. Both are out cold. Still, Dante slowly pulls out the .38 caliber pistol from his belt before creeping toward the bed and the pants crumpled in a ball at the bedside.

Kneeling before the bed, he keeps the gun pointed at Big Jim with his right hand while feeling for the pants pockets with the left. He slips his left hand into the front pocket and feels the large roll of cash. Smiling, he begins to remove his prize, when he feels a vise-like grip around his right hand, forcing the barrel of his pistol downward. Dante hears a click and realizes that the cool metal ring on his forehead is that of a gun barrel—the 9mm Glock of Big Jim.

"You certainly have a lot to learn from the leopard prowling around in the darkness, mate." A naked Big Jim gets out of the bed, yanks the gun out of Dante's hand, and wraps his arm around Dante's neck, half nelson style. "Is this poaching, Miami Beach style?"

"No, Mr. McCullar, it's a fee for services rendered. Now drop your gun."

Big Jim looks over at Marilyn, who's now kneeling on the bed, with her own pistol pointed directly at him.

"Well, aren't you the stealthy lioness of your pride. I never argue with a pretty lady, especially one holding a gun. So I'll just slowly put my gun down now, see."

Continuing to hold Dante in the wrestler's half nelson grip, he squats down to place the gun on the floor, all the time looking straight at Marilyn. As she begins to lower her own weapon, he releases Dante and grabs the bed frame, lifting it just enough to knock her backwards off the bed. He then turns back to Dante and pulls his arm out its socket. With Dante now writhing in pain on the floor, Big Jim circles the bed to pick Marilyn off the floor.

"This one's on me, eh? That was a bad idea. You not only broke our deal, you broke the rules of the hunt. When a lioness fails in a hunt, the pride misses a meal, and she returns with scars that remind her not to fail the next time. Maybe a scar will also teach you a thing or two."

Ignoring her pleas for mercy, Big Jim drags Marilyn over to his belt, and with his free hand, removes one of his knives and runs it across her left cheek. He then releases his grip and turns to get dressed. Marilyn sinks to the floor, sobbing and holding her hand over her left cheek, not so much to catch the bleeding, but to deny the inevitable scar that will end her reign as the most desirable escort in town. Before leaving, Big Jim pulls the whimpering Dante off the floor and throws him onto the bed.

"I don't think you'll want to call the authorities. I'm sure the Miami Beach Chamber of Commerce would take a dim view of your business model."

Big Jim then walks down the hall to the elevator, the alpha male once again.

***

Half a world away from the underbelly of Miami nightlife, Li Chi lies curled up on the bed of her small dormitory room. Just that afternoon, she received the terrible news that her beloved mother is dreadfully ill. One of Li Chi's fellow workers had returned from Li Chi's village on the outskirts of Hong Kong, saying that her mother was bedridden with fever and had a terrible cough.

Li Chi has also grown increasingly worried about her own health, particularly the small black sores on her finger pads and the one on her upper left arm, which she has concealed with a long-sleeved blouse. Not knowing who else to trust, Li Chi finally decides to confide in her roommate, Dow Chin. Dow Chin is seventeen years old and wiser to the workings of the factory and life in general. She also is one of the girls who periodically offers favors to Tang Ma for extra privileges, including permission to visit her family in Hong Kong.

When Dow Chin returns to the dorm, Li Chi tells her of the black sores and is surprised when Dow Chin pulls up her sleeves to reveal that she, too, has developed some black sores on her hands and wrists. In fact, she returned from Hong Kong three days ago with an herbal medicine salve. She shares it with Li Chi, rubbing the light green, gelatinous salve on her sores before administering to her own.

Then, like an older sister speaking to a naïve younger sibling, Dow Chin gently but matter-of-factly advises Li Chi to accept Tang Ma's advances and respectfully ask for time to visit her sick mother. Tang Ma will surely say yes, she explains. For, oddly enough, he feels it would be dishonorable not to pay for his favors. He also wants to ensure he gets more of them in the future.

"But never demand anything from him," Dow Chin warns. "For then he is sure to deny you."

Li Chi thanks her roommate for the salve and the words of advice. As she goes to bed that night, she's still weighing the repulsive thought of giving herself to Tang Ma against the agonizing one that she may never see her mother again.

After a fitful sleep, Li Chi awakes at her usual 5:00 a.m. to get ready for the workday. She's horrified to see that the small black sores are larger and are more numerous. Overwhelmed by a wave of desperation and powerlessness, she resigns herself to please Tang Ma if he flirts with her once again.

Late that afternoon, Tang Ma comes by her station as part of his rounds to check that the girls' work is up to snuff. Sure enough, he firmly places a hand on Li Chi's right shoulder so she'll stop her carving for a moment. He compliments her on her fine workmanship and dedication and how, despite the long working hours, she maintains her beauty and such a positive attitude. The girls at neighboring workstations roll their eyes. They've all heard this line before, and many have taken Tang Ma up on the invitation that will surely follow.

For the first time, Li Chi opens herself up to him by reaching up and placing her left hand over his. Then, with a broad smile and a reverent bow of her head, she compliments him as a smart and strong businessman. Tang Ma rewards her with a slimy grin and invites her up to his office for tea after 6:00 p.m. before proceeding on to another station. Li Chi ignores the knowing smiles of the girls around her and turns back to her work on the ivory, confident that she's doing the right thing for herself and her mother.

Promptly at 6:00, Li Chi climbs the two flights of stairs to Tang Ma's office. With each step, she forces herself to resist the urge to turn around and run back to the dormitory. All too soon, she reaches the top and politely knocks on the door. When Tang Ma answers, she bows her head slowly, a show of respect that barely disguises her revulsion. Tang Ma, a man in his early fifties with a crew cut, stained yellow teeth, and a paunch, is much different than the teenage boys she had crushes on back home and even further from her girlish imaginings of a first lover.

Invited in, she immediately enjoys the cool air of the air conditioning, something she's only experienced once before. She notices a window and is marveled at the sight of birds in an adjacent tree. She inhales the musty smell that's somewhat mitigated by the scent of brewing tea. In fact, she's surprised to find that there's actually tea, rather than just an excuse to lure her to the office.

With a flash of yellow teeth, Tang Ma invites her to sit with him on a large, cool fabric sofa. She smiles at him as he makes his initial move of placing a hand on her skirt at the level of her thigh. She hears Tang Ma talking to her, but she shuts out his words. She feels the cool air touching her breast as she realizes her blouse is unbuttoned. Now in a fog created by her attempts to accept the inevitable while pretending it isn't real, she feels Tang Ma's hot, stale breath as their lips touch and his tongue slips in to meet hers.

She forces down the feelings of panic as she realizes she's being laid down on the sofa pillows and that her thin, brown skirt is being lifted above her waist. Staring blankly ahead, her eyes well with tears as she hears, in the distance, the rustling of clothes then feels her waist being lifted and her underpants pulled down past her ankles.

Fearful of what's about to happen but committed to endure it, she recalls a memory from a few years ago with her beloved mother. They were preparing the family dinner together and talking about life and how things were changing in China. How business and medicine were becoming more privatized and advanced. That women were becoming more accepted in the professions. That someday Li Chi could be a nurse or even a doctor. But that was before she began working in the factory.

Her daydreaming continues even through the pain of the first penetration and the anguish that follows. It continues even as Tang Ma helps her with her clothes and tells her to take the next three days off to visit her family. Shamed but relieved that it's over, and happy that she can now see her mother once again, Li Chi convinces herself that it was all just a bad dream.

CHAPTER 21
Two Epidemics

Peter Fowler, MD, Ph.D., scratches his head as he looks over the data sheets strewn in sections on his conference room table. Fowler, in his mid-fifties, has wavy brown hair and a beard that are just beginning to show speckles of gray. With his glasses, blue shirt with a bow tie, and a checkered vest, he fits the image of a studious professor. However, three weeks after receiving the specimen of anthrax from the patient in Miami, the Director of Communicable Disease at the Centers for Disease Control in Atlanta remains baffled. For in those three weeks, an anthrax epidemic has broken out, not only in China and almost every other Southeast Asian country like Singapore, Malaysia, Vietnam, Japan, and Korea, but also, albeit to a much less degree, in almost every city in Europe and North America.

Alone in his conference room, devoid of windows and with the smell of brewing coffee permeating the air, he rethinks things from the beginning. The first case was an Australian visiting Miami. The specimen clearly showed the anthrax bacillus, a genetically altered one. Then a flood of reports came in from Hong Kong. Of the 197 young Chinese girls working in some type of factory, 172 of them had contracted cutaneous anthrax, as did eight of their supervisors and the owner.

Fowler had received five culture specimens from the treating physicians in Hong Kong. The anthrax bacilli were all the same and were identical to the Miami specimen. After that, reports of less clustered cases throughout China, Singapore, and South Korea seemed to be isolated to the upper and middle classes. Even those similar cases in Europe and North America were mostly in well-to-do Chinese and other Asian individuals.

"The problem is no deaths," Fowler mutters to himself. "Absolutely no deaths. Everyone responds to simple antibiotics."

This anthrax was the more benign cutaneous form, not the more lethal pulmonary and abdominal form. Furthermore, the altered bacteria wasn't the altered, highly virulent and multi-antibiotic-resistant form found in the Soviet Union after the Berlin Wall came down. In fact, it had been altered in the opposite direction, to be less virulent and uniformly sensitive to standard antibiotics. Someone really knew what they were doing with this, but who and why? Was it part of the biological warfare arsenal the former Soviet Union designed to demoralize an enemy or strike fear in them without killing them? Was it more recently developed by Iran and North Korea for the same purpose, or perhaps these wannabe superpowers just didn't know how to make weaponized bacteria? What was the link? And why had it mostly affected Chinese and other Asians?

"I need to find out how each person came into contact with this particular anthrax bacillus."

While Dr. Fowler is trying to put together his infectious disease puzzle, at least enough to present it to the section chief's conference tomorrow, his counterpart in the pharmacology section, Dr. Tsegga Jackson, is dealing with a similar but much more lethal epidemic.

Dr. Jackson is a sixty-year-old black man of medium build with a kind face and, save for some gray hair at the sides, a bald head. Dressed in brown pants and a tan corduroy jacket covering a maroon shirt, he looks more the image of an English professor than a world-renowned scientist.

The son of two diplomats, he was born in Ethiopia and educated in the best private schools, including Yale and John's Hopkins, where he obtained his medical degree and Ph.D. in pharmacology. During his lengthy career, he has won numerous awards for identifying and determining the medical benefits from natural plant extracts and insects. He is proudest, however, of his twenty-five years at the CDC.

Recently, Jackson and his team of three scientists have been working on an ever-growing number of deaths and near-death experiences due to rhino horn powder. It started with four deaths in a brothel in Chicago's Chinatown. Then twin bridegrooms in Miami, both of which were Chinese, and now he's getting a growing number of reports from San Francisco's Chinese and Asian populations, not to mention an even greater number from mainland China and Taiwan.

To Jackson, it's no mystery why Asians, particularly male Chinese, are targeted. They're the main cultures which have historically used rhino horn powder as an aphrodisiac as well as a treatment for other medical conditions. It's their culture's version of an immune booster.

The puzzle is how the Viagra and an inhibitory enzyme got mixed into the powder, and in consistent, well-measured ratios. His testing has determined that the enzyme is a new synthetic, one that inhibits the CPY40 liver enzyme, which normally breaks down many drugs, including Viagra, to prevent them from accumulating to toxic levels. The result is that Viagra has a much more profound effect and lasts a lot longer. In too many cases, the blood divergence to the genital areas is so great that the taker's blood pressure drops too low for far too long, starting a downhill spiral of heart arrhythmias, cardiac arrest, or even a stroke, resulting in death.

Tsegga Jackson concluded that the creation and synthesis of such a sophisticated drug would require the sort of lab that only the pharmaceutical giants of today could afford. Some serious development and planning went into this, and Jackson isn't naïve as to the purpose—market dominance and billions in revenues.

CHAPTER 22
The Tusk Speaks Volumes

Dr. Merriweather is shocked when, two weeks after being released from his quarantine, Big Jim McCullar shows up at his office.

"Well, well, this is unexpected." Merriweather gestures to the chair in front of his desk.

Big Jim chuckles and sets down the large burlap bag he's carrying. "I wanted to stop in and thank you again for curing me."

"No thanks necessary. Just doing my job."

"Big Jim isn't one to forget his friends. I'm off to Joburg, and thanks to you, looking like my old self. But first I wanted to return the favor, and that's why I've brought you this gift." He reaches into the bag and pulls out an object wrapped in cloth. "It's from the tusk of the biggest bull elephant I ever shot. Old George, I called him. I thought it would look good with all those awards on your walls. Hang it with pride, Doc. Old George almost killed me before I got him."

With more words of thanks, Big Jim shakes the hand of Dr. Merriweather and is out the door for his next adventure, totally healed and showing no ill effects from the anthrax or his two-month-long binge on Miami Beach.

Dr. Merriweather removes the opaque bubble wrap to reveal a stunning twelve-inch length of a shiny elephant tusk, ornately trimmed with a gold cap at the base and a metal stud embedded inside to hang it on a wall with perfect balance. Certainly a great gift and worth a tidy sum. However, looking at it, Dr. Merriweather feels only sadness mingled with disgust, aware that it's from the elephant and rhino poaching that has decimated the stocks of these magnificent animals.

He's wondering what he will do with the tusk, when a distant memory flashes through his mind. He turns back to the unpolished tusk tip with a keen eye. Its natural gloss stands out. He stares at it for several minutes trying to remember a medical report he once read about ivory.

"Think, think, Bob. What was it? What was it?"

A moment later, it comes to him—a weekly Morbidity and Mortality Report, now several years old, from the CDC. That report was about a rare case of anthrax in a famous New York pianist who had his piano keys made of imported natural ivory from Africa rather than plastic keys. Crazy as it seemed, it was determined that the anthrax bacillus was hiding in the developmental lines within the ivory. The pianist must've inhaled some of the spores and developed pulmonary anthrax. He later died, earning him the dubious distinction of notoriety in an MMR newsletter from the CDC.

Now, Dr. Merriweather tries to go back even further in

his mind, to his beginnings as a dental student at the now-closed Northwestern University Dental School.

"Come on, Bob. What are those developmental lines in ivory called and where are they? Elephant tusks are teeth. The ivory is merely dentin, just like most of the volume of our own teeth, which are covered by enamel. That's it! Beneath the enamel is our dentin."

Dr. Merriweather rips off the gold cap at the base of his gift to reveal the cut stump of the tusk, where the enamel has been removed and the dentin cut across. There they are, the developmental lines he now recalls as Schreger lines, which he learned in his comparative dental anatomy class many years ago. Such Schreger lines are seen as the cross-hatchings on the butt of a sawn-off tusk and worn surfaces of the tusk, much like the growth rings on a tree trunk.

Merriweather reaches for some blue gloves in a box behind his desk to protect him from what he fears may be in those Schreger lines. He then puts on the magnifying lenses he uses to suture fine nerves and blood vessels. Within the lines, within the tusks, he can make out brownish debris.

"Could this be the source of Big Jim's anthrax?"

He leaves the offices and heads to the sterile instrument section of his clinic. There, he picks up the finest point dental explorer he can find and a sterile test tube. He manages to scrape some of the debris out of the deeper positioned Schreger lines and some from the glossy surface of the tusk, keeping the two samples separate. Then, like a child with a new find, he rushes off to Rebecca Palmer's pathology lab.

"Rebecca, can your lab people do a thin smear and slide for a Gram stain on these two specimens, separately? I got it from an elephant's tusk that Big Jim gave me. This might be the source of his anthrax."

Dr. Palmer takes it to her lab technicians for the microscopic slides, a Gram stain, and a formal culture. After just five minutes, the anxious duo looks at the superficial debris slide first. Using her two-headed microscope, they view the slide simultaneously. An immediate sense of discovery comes over them as they can clearly see the numerous Gram-positive rods, highly suspicious for bacillus anthrax, on the slide from the glossy surface. They look at the slide from the deeper debris specimen. No such bacteria are seen.

"Rebecca, do you know what this means? The anthrax bacillus isn't natural. It didn't get incorporated into the tusk properly. It must've been acquired recently, or someone must've put it on the tusk purposely."

For a moment, the two stare at each other in silence, then Rebecca begins searching for the phone number of Peter Fowler at the CDC. She doesn't get through to him, though. It seems Dr. Fowler is at a joint meeting of section chiefs, reporting what he can about a mysterious anthrax outbreak.

CHAPTER 23
Two Meetings

It takes several days of phone tag before Rebecca Palmer and Peter Fowler connect, and another day for the culture specimens to arrive at Fowler's lab. He has since confirmed that the anthrax bacillus from the surface of Old George's tusk is indeed the same altered form contracted by Big Jim and several other cases he's reviewed. His research has also discovered that the many others who developed anthrax also had contact with some form of ivory from Africa, and that the factory girls in Hong Kong were all working with ivory. There's now no doubt that the link is ivory from Africa. However, that the genetic alteration is a less virulent form continues to trouble him. Is it the work of some mastermind in infectious disease? If so, for what earthly purpose? More likely, it's a natural zoonosis, the kind he's seen in the wild many times and which caused the evolution of Ebola virus and SARS of recent years. *Yes, that's it—a zoonosis*, not one to ascribe to conspiracy theories.

Tsegga Jackson is also trying to rationalize his epidemic. He accepts that distributors of rhino horn powder add Viagra and other erectile enhancers to the powdered horn to add credence to its lore. But how do these distributors get a synthetic enzyme that adds potency and duration to the drug? One that takes the most up-to-date biomedical technology and pharmacologic knowledge to create. He has no specific answer.

After meeting with the Director of the CDC, Jackson and Fowler leave dismayed. They each hoped to gain encouragement and the financial support they'd need to continue pursuing their medical detective work. For Fowler, the kind of support necessary to trace the source of the infection vector of the ivory. For Jackson, the kind of support necessary to find the group that synthesized the enzyme that allows the Viagra's effect to be stronger and last longer. Instead, they were told to craft a politically correct medical alert for distribution through the American Medical Association, the European Medical Association, and the World Health Organization.

Fowler was reminded that although an anthrax epidemic would normally be an international concern, this one was only related to an illegal ivory trade, something that can't be controlled due to the political and economic limitations within the countries involved. Besides, no deaths have occurred, and the strain of anthrax bacillus wasn't the feared weaponized strain of the Cold War. He was further reminded that the tone of his medical alert shouldn't be of the sort that creates a worldwide panic.

Dr. Jackson was reminded that although the deaths attributed to this diabolical addition to rhino horn powder was concerning, it was limited to only a culture that believes in the false medical benefits from an otherwise inert ingredient. Once its patrons realize the new danger in using powdered rhino horn, they will stop using it, and by word of mouth, others will be tempted to do the same. The problem will self-correct.

"Put out your medical alert warnings and get the WHO to do the same," the CDC Director tells the frustrated scientists. "Then devote all your efforts to the ZIKA virus concerns that are permeating through our political community. Remember who funds us."

***

Two weeks after the CDC and WHO medical alerts hit the international medical community and, worse, social media, David Epstein, CEO of Apollo Pharmaceuticals, convenes a secret meeting with his Director of Research, Richard Bloom, and his Director of International Marketing, Robert Malmo.

"Gentlemen, it looks like our little experiment has worked."

"Worked? David, how can you say that? I've read about the deaths reported by the Centers for Disease Control. A bunch of Asians have already died, and more are likely to follow. All from the additive I gave to Chang Li in Johannesburg six months ago."

"Calm down, Robert. Those superstitious people shouldn't have been sniffing powdered rhino horn anyway. The experiment was a success. Wouldn't you say, Richard?"

"In terms of our goal, yes. Enzyme U-515 successfully inhibited the breakdown of sildenafil, making it more potent and longer lasting. It will likely do the same for high blood pressure meds, cholesterol-lowering drugs, and painkillers, among others. If we can just get the dose right, it'll be our next multibillion-dollar blockbuster drug. Maybe the first multitrillion-dollar blockbuster drug. We'll be able to enhance the effect and duration of most every drug now on the market. We'll have the patent, and every other company will have to come to us."

"You see, Robert," David Epstein says, "we now know that enzyme U-515 works on humans. We bypassed ten years of preclinical trials on animals. PETA would be proud of us, wouldn't you say, Richard?" He looks at Bloom.

The two men exchange a smug chuckle.

"Richard, I need you to do two things now. First, fabricate some animal study data to convince the FDA that we've been doing preclinical animal studies all along. Make it sound extensive across several animal models but no companion animals like dogs or cats. We don't want any outraged pet lovers demanding an investigation. Use rats, rabbits, and pigs, and make it sound believable. Second, adjust the dose so that we don't get these damned overdose side effects."

Robert Malmo keeps up appearances, but his gut is roiling with disgust for Bloom and Epstein … and for himself. On his trip to Simbambili, he saw the other side of this—a side where poachers are eaten by lions and whole species are threatened with extinction. A side well beyond the bottom line.

Malmo leaves the meeting with an intent to resign and seek a position outside the pharmaceutical industry. He never thought it would come to this, but now that it has, he can't turn back. He briefly contemplates going to the press, becoming a whistle-blower but dismisses it quickly, afraid of retribution or being blackballed from other employment, or worse. No, he must be pragmatic. He must think about Kimberly and Angela. He'll wait six months then advance a family need to cut down on his traveling so as not to make it seem connected to this unethical project.

After Malmo leaves, Epstein and Bloom begin the task of projecting enhanced revenues from the drugs in their drug portfolio. All will be marketed as more effective and longer lasting.

"We'll deal with the side effects later, as we always do," Epstein concludes.

CHAPTER 24
The Market Correction

Six months later, the CDC has been proven right. The cases of mild anthrax have subsided. There has been only a rare incidence of deaths from rhino horn powder, all attributed to stocks from older batches. Fowler and Tsegga have indeed moved on to study the Zika virus epidemic but regret that they're still unable to explain how it started and why it ended.

Chang Li looks over his empty Johannesburg warehouse. Of his eleven employees, only Graphite Persus remains, and he's more of a caretaker and security guard now. Gone also are the boxes of vials for powdered rhino horn, the grinding lathes, the shipping labels, and other accoutrements of his former lab. As implied by the Director of the CDC, his distributors in China and elsewhere in Asia now have no customers. Everyone is afraid of using the rhino horn powder. It's poison, they say.

"Stupid, ignorant people," Chang Li mutters. "Hunters don't even want to kill rhinos anymore. No demand, no supply." He sighs.

Now, what is he going to do with this building? He could turn it into a restaurant. Perhaps rent it out? But to who?

Maybe a casino. "That's it. A casino, just like Las Vegas."

At 8:00 a.m. in Hong Kong, Tang Ma is now in hiding. No one wants ivory anymore either. The landlord of the toy factory has put out a hit on him. Most of his girls developed anthrax, and even though they've all healed, it cost him a pretty penny for their medical care and loss of work. Now, the warehouse is thought to be a sick building. No one wants to work there. His landlord can't rent it out to anyone else, hence the price on Tang Ma's head. Tang Ma's well-to-do clients have abandoned him as well. Now holed up in the backroom of a deserted machine shop, he's unable to get to the money he has left. Even if he did make it to the hiding place alive, the Chinese Mafia would be waiting for him there. Even his family is afraid and refusing to help. He has no one.

Hungry, stir-crazy, and desperate, Tang Ma decides to chance it. He puts on a makeshift disguise of glasses and a baseball cap, thinking he'll get lost in the crowded streets of Hong Kong. He leaves the machine shop, carrying a box to mimic that of a worker. As he gets to the throngs of people and rickshaws, he discards the box and walks with his head down, trying to position himself between larger people and vehicles to be less noticeable. He knows the general direction of the loading docks by the harbor.

After several hours of back switches and entering storefronts and slipping out the back, he's confident no one has followed him. Arriving at the shipping docks, in a twist of irony, he sees the familiar cargo ship the *Dragon Master*. He uses his last yuan to bribe an old acquaintance, the harbor master, to let him aboard and secure his secret.

The ship is now desolate except for a contingency crew of five, all sleeping or doing mundane chores elsewhere. He sneaks down to the engine room. It's not too comfortable, but he doesn't care. The *Dragon Master* is due to leave the docks tomorrow, and he'll be safe.

In Miami, it's 8:00 p.m., and a weary Dr. Merriweather is dictating his second surgery of the day. It lasted longer than expected but turned out as he wanted. Clear margins on a cancer resection of the tongue, and a viable tissue flap reconstruction by his former fellow and now co-faculty Dr. Torborg. As he signs off on his dictation, he looks over to his cell phone loudly quacking to get his attention.

"Are you Dr. Merriweather?" a voice asks.

"Yes, what can I do for you?"

"This is Officer Punales from Coral Gables Police. We are at the home of a Mr. Frank Eng, and, Doctor, we have a situation here. Mr. Eng is in his living room, threatening suicide. His wife asked us to call you. She thinks you might be able to help. He's got a gun up to his head."

Dr. Merriweather closes his eyes. *Frank, no.*

"Dr. Merriweather?"

"Yes, Officer, I'll be there right away. Yes, I know the address. See you in fifteen."

Dr. Merriweather tears out of his office and into a quiet and balmy South Florida night, already pulling out the remote starter. He slides in and peels out of the parking lot, screeching tires for the first time since he was a teenager driving his dad's '58 Chevrolet. He speeds down US-1 to Ponce De Leon Boulevard, running two stoplights on the way. As he arrives at the Eng house, on Ponce de Leon Avenue, he sees the flashing lights of two police cars, one on the lawn and another in the driveway. He can also see the front door open and someone in the doorway he suspects is a professional suicide negotiator talking pointedly, probably to Frank Eng, in the living room.

Once he gets out of his car, he's held back by another officer thinking he's one of the curious neighbors and bystanders gathered around on adjacent front lawns. A sobbing Vivian Eng runs over and manages to explain to the officer that she wants him there. Dr. Merriweather embraces the woman, and before he can ask what's happened, she tells him that Frank has been blaming himself for the deaths of his two sons more and more over the past several weeks.

"He doesn't sleep, and he's been spending hours each day at their gravesites. Today, he sat on the sofa all afternoon just staring straight ahead, muttering to himself. I tried to talk to him. I told him that our sons wouldn't want him to feel this way. They wouldn't want him to throw his own life away. An hour ago, he put a gun to his head and told me to go away or he'd pull the trigger. Dr. Merriweather, I didn't even know he owned a gun! The police have been talking to him for the past hour. Every time they try to enter, he yells at them to stand back or he'll shoot. Dr. Merriweather, you know him, and you knew my sons. He respects you. Maybe you can—"

Before she can finish, they hear a *pop* that sounds like a firecracker, but both of them know. They rush toward the door to find the negotiator now holding the man he unsuccessfully tried to talk out of suicide. The sobbing wife replaces the negotiator to hug her fallen husband, who has blood oozing out of his right temple.

The remaining officers rush into the living room to find Merriweather and the negotiator hugging Mrs. Eng as she holds tightly to the limp and lifeless body of her husband. The enormity of this family tragedy is almost enough to bring Merriweather to his knees.

At the same time, in Hong Kong, the Harbor Patrol pulls a floating body out of the water. It's Tang Ma with three bullet holes in the back of his head. Certainly an execution, they say. It seems the harbor master is also a master of the better deal. Unlike Mr. Eng, no one will be crying over Tang Ma's lifeless body.

✳✳✳

Fate has been much kinder to Li Chi. Her three days off coincided with the outbreak of cutaneous anthrax among the workers and supervisors in her factory, causing it to close. She never returned. Her own black sores responded to the pills her Hong Kong doctors gave her and, in just one week, completely disappeared. She doesn't know the name of the pills, just that they were different than the ones her mother took for what the doctors called an acquired pneumonia.

Both she and her mother are well again and, more importantly, back together again. Now fifteen, she goes to school, a pre-nursing program she learned about while her mother was in the hospital. She still works, though the combined hours of school and work is less than what she put in at that awful factory each day. She lied about her age to qualify for a work permit in the licensed restaurant just five minutes from the small home she shares with her mother. The years of work in the toy factory and the ivory carving are now just a fading memory. Even the painful ordeal with Tang Ma just seems like the bad dream she hoped it would be. She's happy now for the first time in three years. She even flirts occasionally with a boy in her pre-nursing class. Nothing serious as of yet, but who knows?

At Apollo Pharmaceuticals, David Epstein and Richard Bloom are also envisioning a bright future, albeit one of a very different kind. They have just been approved by the FDA for eight human trials of enzyme U-515. The good news didn't come without hard work, though. In fact, Richard Bloom had personally fabricated over a thousand pages of research depicting three preclinical animal studies, each with an elaborate statistical analysis proving the safety and efficacy of the enzyme. He even purchased rats, pigs, and nonhuman primates to create a paper trail and image of a serious preclinical effort. Of course, he changed the purchase dates on the invoices to span an eight-year period to prove to the FDA that their studies were rigorous and escalated over time. What happened to the animals? Some were used for other less important projects, while others were merely sacrificed on arrival.

Today, they're toasting their plan to fast-track U-515 through the FDA and beat out all their competitors in the race for more potent and longer-lasting drugs. They even hope to put a few of the smaller drug companies and startups out of business. After all, gobbling up the weak is just as common in corporate boardrooms as it is in the African bush, and it's probably more vicious.

CHAPTER 25
A Revelation

With the anthrax epidemic under control, Robert Merriweather knows he should be relieved, even pleased with himself for making the discovery on Big Jim's tusk. Yet he's neither. In fact, as the weeks go on, he finds himself unable to think of much else. He simply can't shake the thought that one of his old corporate enemies might be behind the rhino horn powder deaths.

He knows that only a drug company with sophisticated equipment and paid expertise could possibly develop an enzyme that blocks the body's ability to metabolize and rid itself of medications and worse, natural toxins from normal metabolism or from things eaten. Did they even think of such unintended consequences?

"Of course not," he mutters. "They certainly didn't when they covered up the effects of their cis-phosphorus drugs, namely, murderous psychotic behavior. They also didn't consider that natural marine toxins in low doses, which could render a state of suspended animation, would also turn those who received them into murderous zombies."

Dr. Merriweather breaks away from his early morning introspection to head to the pre-op area and prepare his first case, a midface and jaw fracture that will certainly require several titanium plates. As he races through the surgeon's lounge, he's met by Rick Casaeres, the local instrument representative of the KLS Medical Device Company. It's not unusual for him to see Rick prior to a case and inform him of the number and sizes of the plates he intends to use in each case. In fact, Dr. Merriweather has known Rick Casaeres for more than ten years and prefers the design and precise workmanship of the KLS system.

However, he's shocked when he sees Casaeres speaking with none other than Robert Malmo.

"Bob M-1, great to see you! What're you doing here?"

Malmo glances at Casaeres expectantly.

"Robert Malmo is our new district regional manager. He started a month ago and has been making the rounds of our top users. I didn't know you knew each other."

"That's all right, Rick, Mr. Malmo here and I go back a few months. Shall we say, to a rather eventful trip to the Simbambili Safari Camp in South Africa. If you'll excuse us, let me and Mr. Malmo get reacquainted here."

Dr. Merriweather asks his chief resident to get the patient ready for the surgery and let the family know that he'll be along shortly. He and Malmo then move to an unoccupied conference room to talk further.

"Robert, I'm glad to see you're not with Apollo Pharmaceuticals anymore. But I must ask, why'd you change? The timing seems a little ... suspicious."

Malmo smiles, but he avoids Robert's eyes. "Suspicious? How so?"

"Well, after putting everything together about the deaths related to rhino powder, and the sophisticated science behind making an enzyme additive that prolongs drug effects, it all seems eerily reminiscent of my previous experience with Apollo."

Robert Malmo opens his mouth, ready to give Merriweather his canned response to any questions about his departure from Apollo, then he just shrugs. "Okay, you deserve to know the truth, Bob M-1. You're right. Apollo produced the enzyme and used it together with Viagra in the rhino horn powder to test it on humans. The budget they put up for it was enormous. I guess I turned a blind eye to the possible consequences of the project due to the large bonuses I got. By testing it with the rhino horn powder, they avoided a direct connection to Apollo and at the same time leapfrogged over eight years of required studies on animals. They've hoodwinked the FDA so far, as they have in the past, and plan to apply it to almost every other drug in their listings, and even license it to other pharmaceutical companies for a tidy sum. All the deaths from the Viagra overdoses don't even seem to faze them. That's when I decided to leave. I hope you understand and don't hold it against me for working for them."

"No, I most certainly don't. In fact, I respect you for your decision to leave the company. Sadly, I suspect they'll get away with it. I know they cover their tracks better than any criminal organization. I hope, maybe with your help, that we can someday expose them for what and who they are."

CHAPTER 26
Supply and Demand

In the Sabi Sands Game Reserve, near the southern end of Kruger National Park in South Africa, a male white rhino approaches an old, seldom-used midden. At five years of age, he's just now entering his prime. Perhaps due to the notoriously poor eyesight of the rhinoceros, or to his focus on an enticing new scent in the midden, he takes no notice of a huge skull with the front of the face missing, a previous fallen rhino visitor to the midden, now long since forgotten. However, for this young rhino, there's no threat from a bullet. No one covets his two stately horns. Gone now are the local poachers eager to discard their country's heritage to sustain their own living. Gone now are the great white hunters eager for trophies or for profits. Gone also are the middlemen and distributors. But more importantly, gone are all the customers for rhino horns. The cultures that once coveted the gray powder for not only sexual enhancement but for a myriad of medical ills now believe it to be a poison that will kill you.

This young male is oblivious to all that has changed. His singular focus is on the strange and enticing scent in the midden. It's the scent of estrogen. A similarly aged female rhino visited the midden recently. He's stimulated to spread his own chemical message of desire. He kicks the clumps of dung and defecates his own together with a spray of pheromones, just like Goliath had done over a year ago. As he moves off the midden, he relies on his nose and his heightened senses to track the female in heat. He and a few others of his kind hold the hope for the future of rhinos by following their instincts played out over the past sixty thousand years.

***

The annual cycle of elephant migrations brings the matriarch and her herd back to the Uganda clearing where Big Jim ravaged her sisters, cousins, and daughters. Although her herd is smaller than last year, six of her ten surviving adults are pregnant. She herself is carrying the remaining genes of Old George, now sixteen months into her twenty-two-month gestation. If she were human, she would be showing her pregnancy, but in elephants, who can tell?

She and her herd break off tree limbs and slowly chew the bark and tender leaves before plodding into the area of the clearing Big Jim designated as the kill zone. There, they linger and gather together. Each one gently caresses the white bones scattered across the field with their trunks. Occasionally, one lifts a bone to then gently lay it down again. There seems to be a purpose for this type of gathering, but no human has been able to figure it out except that it's their obvious respect for their dead loved ones. The touching and caressing continues for more than twenty minutes before the matriarch signals a respectful and quiet conclusion. She gives a low rumble, which signals them to follow her. The instincts of leading the herd to the life-sustaining water of the river is the priority now that they've paid their respects to the dead.

They pass by the tree where Big Jim once sat, perched to get off his kill shots and ponder his unfortunate childhood—the past that led him to become the remorseless hunter he was. Today, there are no kill shots. There haven't been any in more than a year now. Gone is Nobutu Ingale. Gone is his Revolution Liberations Army. Gone is Big Jim McCullar. Ivory today isn't wanted. It brings disease. It's said that elephants carry bad germs in their tusks. They're safe for now.

At 10:00 a.m. in Miami, Dr. Merriweather sits behind his office desk, staring at the chart on the computer screen in front of him. His thoughts are about Frank Eng and his two sons, Mark and Michael, all three now dead. From Robert Malmo, his suspicions that an additive to the Viagra in the powdered rhino horn was the catalyst of the tragedies that followed, and that Apollo Pharmaceuticals engineered the heightened and prolonged drug effects, are now confirmed. The same company he testified against in the Bone Protect scandal two years ago, and those behind the corruption of his old anesthesiologist friend, Dr. Saltzman. However, Robert isn't comforted by the knowledge. He's only filled with the helplessness that he can't prove it.

Despite his contributions to the finding of an altered anthrax bacillus from the Old George ivory tusk given to him as an appreciation gift from Big Jim McCullar, he's unaware of its origin and of its significance. He, like most others, attributes it to a natural mutation. Since the CDC has dropped its investigation, it appears this, too, will remain a mystery.

And yet, as frustrated as he is by these unanswered questions, he also finds them a welcome distraction from those in his personal life—those surrounding Heather Bellaire. Then again, if the death of the Engs and the rhino conundrum have shown him anything, it's that not all questions have answers. Maybe it just is what it is. He makes a personal commitment right then.

***

At 5:00 p.m. in Witwatersrand's Hospital in Johannesburg, Professor Randall Lurie is just completing his graduate seminar for his eight microbiology graduate students. As today's droll discussion concerning the life cycle of the parasite that causes malaria concludes, one of his students shows the professor the third page of the *Johannesburg Times* newspaper. Although already aware of what it says, Professor Lurie humors his student and reads the passage header aloud:

"Recent Wildlife Census Encouraging."

He then reads the following short passage:

"Although the census for lion continues to decline at an alarming rate, the numbers for the remaining members of

the big five have stabilized for the leopard and buffalo, while the numbers of rhino increased by a modest six percent, and that for the elephant by eight percent. Such good news for the rhinoceros and elephant can be attributed to the global decline in the demand for the rhino horn and for ivory, while the leopard and buffalo stability can be attributed to a good rainy season and the maintenance of their habitat by restrictions on farming."

Professor Lurie smiles broadly at the student who brought him the newspaper and several others who linger.

"You see, there is hope for the very thing that makes our country unique. Here, Mother Nature intervened for us, creating a contamination in the rhino horns and also in the ivory so that no one wants them anymore. But in the future, your generation must take steps to preserve our heritage and not rely on Mother Nature, just like mine has done."

"Professor, there are rumors that it was not mother nature but some activist groups that actually poisoned or purposely caused the contaminations of the elephant tusks and rhino horn."

Professor Lurie, adopting an almost grandfatherly demeanor, retorts, "That would be impossible to do. Preposterous, nothing but another conspiracy theory."

After dismissing his graduate students, Professor Lurie places his notes in a small briefcase and closes the door. He leans back in his office chair, reflecting on the student's comment and the upturn in the numbers for rhinos and elephants with a sense of personal satisfaction. He also realizes a great sense of accomplishment—not to mention relief—that his plan to be captured by Nobutu had worked. It had been dangerous, nearly costing him his life, but how else would he have been able to contaminate the ivory with his attenuated strain of anthrax bacillus? He ponders about how the same concept, so simple concerning supply and demand, might also apply to the illegal drug trade in opium, now causing numerous overdose deaths and addictions in South Africa, as it has done in the United States.

Yes, supply and demand, the age-old axiom of economics. The first degree I earned before entering medical school. How well it works to this very day.

His gaze falls upon the spray bottles marked as "disinfectant," but containing his attenuated anthrax bacteria in his own liquid culture medium stored on an upper shelf in his office. He contemplates destroying the evidence then dismisses the thought, partly out of a certain love for his creation, and partly because he might need to use it again. His mind then briefly contemplates how he or the next generation of concerned scientists could contaminate the cocaine-producing coca plants of South America, or the heroin-producing poppy fields of the Middle East, to reduce the demand for these drugs. Then the reality of the rhino horn deaths hits him. Yes, what about the contamination of the rhino horns? He didn't engineer that one. Who did? That was certainly more serious and even fatal. Was that the hand of cruel Mother Nature, or was it another more sinister version of himself?

Realizing there are no answers to these questions, he gets up, turns off the lights, and closes his door to enter the third-floor hallway of the hospital, which leads to the parking lot. He strolls down the hallway, past the rooms housing patients, with a continued sense of satisfaction. His daydreaming ends as he approaches the nursing station, where the chief nurse behind the computer-clustered desk shouts out a gleeful, "Hello, my good professor!"

Obliged to return the greeting, he turns to respond but stops before he can utter a word. He notices a familiar name on one of the charts behind her—James Francis McCullar. Could it be? Here in the infectious disease ward of his hospital?

Professor Lurie finally returns a short, "Nice to see you," to the nurse while he moves into the station to grab hold of the chart. It reads, *Bed 312: Isolation Precautions required*. His curiosity piqued, he ignores the nursing staff milling about and walks down the hall with the chart tucked under his arm. He dons the yellow personal protective equipment gown, known as a PPE, including a cap and mask, before entering the room.

As he stands at the foot of the bed, in front of him lies a man he doesn't recognize. The man doesn't recognize him either due to the gown and mask he's wearing. This man, although about the same height as Big Jim McCullar, is thin and wasted. His cheeks and eyes are sunken in. The outline of his bones, particularly those of the cheekbones, skull, and fingers, can be seen beneath pale and dry skin. The man has a short, scraggly beard. Even though the hospital staff has tried to shave him once a week, he has fought them tooth and nail. The beard is stained yellow with food remnants and some drool as well.

He looks cadaveric. This can't be the robust Big Jim McCullar I knew in Uganda.

He then sees the Aussie-style hat with the brim turned up on one side next to him on the bed.

Professor Lurie hesitates but gives in to his curiosity. "Mr. McCullar, did you ever know a man named Nobutu Ingale?"

Slow to answer and in a raspy voice, gesturing with a shaky right hand and not recognizing his old roommate, the man answers. "Yeah, I killed the bastard. He tried to kill me and an old professor with black mambas. He got what was coming to him."

Exhausted, even by the effort to speak, the man now identified as the real Big Jim McCullar sinks back into the bed and closes his eyes.

Professor Lurie frantically pages through the chart, guessing and second-guessing to himself.

Did Big Jim contract the more fatal pulmonary form of anthrax? Did my anthrax bacillus mutate to a more virulent form? Oh, my God. If it did, will all the others who now seem to be cured and healed go on to develop the pulmonary form? Oh, my heavens. Did my plan go so very, very wrong just when I thought it worked so perfectly well?

Professor Lurie, continues to frantically page through the

chart. He reads: *CD4 cell count 22/dl, viral load 4 million copies.*

"A virus, not anthrax. Anthrax is a bacterium."

The next page contains the answer he seeks. *Diagnosis: Advanced AIDS. Terminal, Do Not Resuscitate (DNR).*

"Godspeed, Big Jim," Professor Lurie whispers.

As he leaves the room, he remembers the many elephants Big Jim had slain.

We really do reap what we sew. It's just the law of nature.